mother to a stranger
leland bardwell

THE
BLACKSTAFF
PRESS

BELFAST

I would like to thank Mary Branley and Maggie Wade
for their unfailing encouragement.

First published in 2002 by
Blackstaff Press Limited
Wildflower Way, Apollo Road
Belfast BT12 6TA
with the assistance of
The Arts Council of Northern Ireland

ARTS
COUNCIL
of Northern Ireland

Typeset by Techniset Typesetters, Newton-le-Willows, Merseyside

Printed in Ireland by ColourBooks Ltd

A CIP catalogue record for this book
is available from the British Library

ISBN 0-85640-716-X

www.blackstaffpress.com

for my extended family

PART I

THE LETTER WAS HEADED 'Messrs Forbes and Bell, solicitors', and was from somewhere called Crowsfort, in Surrey, England.

'Dear Mrs McDonald,' she read, '. . . it has now been proven beyond doubt . . .'

Her gaze raced through the typed words . . . Dear God, no. She had expected a bill, an invitation, a reminder. Anything but this.

She wanted to call the postman back. Tell him the letter was meant for someone else. They had got the names mixed. McDonald was a common name. She read it again. Yes, it was there. All there. Place, date, even the time, correct to the last minute.

She took several turns around the lawn, looking nervously at the house. She could see Jim behind the kitchen window, leaning over the sink. As he looked up, he saw her and smiled.

She unlatched the door of the henhouse and the birds raced out with a scatter of feathers as she gave them their meal.

Dear God! No!

Jim was probably making the coffee. A morning ritual. Like prayers.

He called her. And again: 'Nan, what's keeping you? Coffee's made.'

She went through the back door into the kitchen.

He gave her a hug. 'What's got into you, feeding the hens?'

'Just thought.'

'Do you want a fry?'

'No.'

He looked curiously at her, his two hands on her shoulders. 'What's up?'

'Nothing.'

'You could fool me.'

He switched off the radio. The temperature at Baldonnell yesterday had been 31°C, a record for the month of May. Everyone discussed the weather – in the shops, the pub, the street. Farmers lolled about bare-chested in straw hats, like 1950s movie stars in America's Deep South.

He had never felt happier. Life was perfect. They had spent the morning squealing with laughter until, soaked in sweat, the sheets roped round their feet, they'd had to get up.

'Pity you have to go to Kraków next week. We should be at the seaside. We could have gone to Rosses Point.'

'Rosses Point?'

'Stop footling.' She had begun to pull things around on the dresser. 'What's got into you?'

'Do you really want to know?'

He stared at his wife, standing crooked, one hand clutched in her hair. She didn't look right, somehow. And before he could answer, she began muttering about illegitimate children and fallen women and what it was like having a baby in the 1960s when there was nothing available, only backstreet abortions or suicide.

'In the name of God! Are you telling me that you had a baby?'

'That's what I'm telling you.'

'A baby! That's impossible.'

They'd known each other for years. There wasn't room for this kind of happening.

Was the heat affecting her? He tried to tell her about the temperature in Baldonnell but she screamed at him to shut up and listen.

'He wants to meet me. He's traced me.'

'He?'

'Yes, he. The baby. I've just told you. I registered him as Séan Wine. He was adopted.'

'Where?' As if it mattered.

'In England.'

'In England?'

'In England.' She gave him the letter.

'But why . . .'

Why what? Why hadn't she told him years ago? When he asked her, she shrugged and said he would have left her if he'd known.

'Hold on a minute.'

He tried to catch her hand, but she brushed past him and was out the door again. He gazed after her. Would he? Have left her . . . Of course not! The very idea!

He began to read:

Dear Mrs McDonald

A Mr Charles Henry Fordson has instructed us to
instigate a search and we think that it has now been
proven beyond doubt that Mr Fordson was born Séan
Wine in Cheapside, London, son of Nan Wine . . .
subsequently adopted by a Mr and Mrs Fordson in the
village of Crowsfort in the county of Surrey . . . Nan
Wine, later married to Jim McDonald, in Dublin . . .
He wishes to contact . . .

There was more information, date of birth, et cetera.

Jesus! Why, that's thirty years ago. And where was he then? Thirty years ago . . .

Would he have been walking down Leeson Street towards Earlsfort Terrace? Would he have gone into Dwyer's pub for a pint? How on earth? He couldn't help thinking of Harry the barman, a man in his fifties who had once told him how he had impure thoughts at night and prayed for the thoughts to be taken away.

Impure thoughts!

But thirty years ago?

He would have been at school. Only sixteen. Still the anonymous son of Joe McDonald and his wife, Maura, and grandson of Willie McVeigh, the postman in Shankill, County Wicklow.

And Nanny Wine? My God. She was only a child when she . . .

In England? He looked at the letter again. London. Jesus.

And then . . .

He decided to take a shower. After all, it only is — was — a baby. And now this . . . this man wants . . .

He must go back. Go back. Dig right down to those nuggets they used to share. But there seemed to be a gap. A few years.

He would work it out. He would settle. Count the years. Make a stand. So it all began a few years later. There must have been about three years in between then and later, when it was Nanny Wine everywhere.

He looked out the window silently as his thoughts tunnelled back through time. He wished she would come in and talk sensibly but she had disappeared and the lawn was empty, save for a hen who was having a dust bath in the corner . . .

She had been ogled and crowded, that was for sure. For her seductive terracotta eyes, for her heavy arms that dimpled above the elbows, for her hair scattered on her head like blackberries. Always dashing to the Academy in Westland

Row. Always late. She was waitressing to pay for her music lessons, had digs somewhere. Their first date at the Metropole Cinema.

What was the name of the picture? He racked his brains. They didn't touch for ages. He remembered that. And then hours in the telephone kiosk at the foot of Earlsfort Terrace, where they all tapped out the numbers for free. Skipping his lectures. Jesus. And all the time there had been this ... this thing that had happened. Before they'd even met. And she'd never told him.

And so they'd married in a mist of ignorance, had they? But hadn't he been mad for her? Wild to get married, terrified one of those other shites would scoop her up. In St Brigid's, it was. What a skite and that smart aleck, Justin, saying she looked like a Goya. Fuck him anyhow, inferring that he, Jim, the post-man's grandson, wouldn't even know what a Goya was. Deliberately tried to make him feel a weed in his zoot suit, with his hair all plastered down. But it didn't matter what anyone said. His happiness had made him delirious.

Nan wandered away. She felt heady, inconsequential. Was what had been hidden in the pigeonhole of her brain for so long now going to be thrown into a heap of gossip? And the unsubtle way she'd broken the news to Jim! Why hadn't she waited, till they were in bed perhaps? Gone bit by bit. Was she daft or what? But her judgement had been astray. She'd presented him with a grown-up stranger out of the blue. Her own flesh and blood. How did she expect him to react?

And yet ... Memory plays a callous game. Writes itself into the brain with indelible ink. A falciform awning over the cradle. All ribbons and bows. Blue-for-a-boy ribbons, they'd decked it out, his adoptive parents. And how his face had puckered when Miss Charity picked him up to take him through that door. The door of that dingy hostel where she'd spent the previous month. To present him to that mister and missus, oh so respectable, so middle class, so well got. And Miss Charity had sneered, 'You're an uncaring slut,' and that he'd now have a chance. A chance! Like in a lottery.

She was walking fast on the dusty dried-up headland as she skirted Slater's field. She could hear the hum of Foncie's tractor over the brae. He was cutting and bailing the meadow. Above her the sky shone pale as a bone, the swallows knifing back and forth. Everything normal. Open . . .

She thought of her father. That tall, kindly Jew with those long fingers, that carved sunburnt face under a white thatch of hair. A Mediterranean look on him. And the lies she had told him. That she had a job in England where she could pay for her studies in a famous music college. And he had said, 'But why, why?' And she'd gone, literally run away. Taken the bus to Dun Laoghaire and, sick in her pregnancy, had stood on the rail of the mail boat watching Dublin Bay recede into the horizon. At least, thank God, *he* had never had to suffer this knowledge.

She'd go down to Carr's lake . . . She began to run. But why hadn't she told Jim that time at the Metropole? Would it really have wrecked him? He was so young then. They were both so young. He'd have been horrified. She remembered the sort of things their gang used to say about women who slept around. 'Well used to harness,' was one of them. And that was one of the more savoury expressions! Yuk! What a crowd of luder-amahns! And all so precious underneath! The so-called permissive society! Anyway, what's this the name of the picture they'd seen? Why couldn't she remember? But she could remember lots of other things. Especially in the tea rooms afterwards, and how extraordinary he seemed when he bent down to pick up a spoon and how it was all she could do not to stroke his ears. They were so neat.

But she had never intended to tell anyone. Why should she have? There was no way they could find out. Yet she remembered how the stamp of terror had seldom left her. There had always been that niggling fear that someone might appear and recognise her – someone from that London year. Then as time went on her worries had eased. Wasn't she doing the one thing that she had always wanted to do, her chosen career, assured? Nothing was going to get in her way.

And there was Jim and his laughter. The way his shoulders moved independently of each other like rabbits. The way the pupils of his eyes swivelled when he was struck by some comic incident.

Everything had seemed to slot into place as all that following year they did a serious line. Did a line! What an expression ... And to think that that was the time of the condom war, when the Catholic hierarchy threw the Robinson Bill out the window! But there was always the chemist at the corner of Merrion Row, well known for under-the-counter dealing, so after some weeks of frantic petting they had jumped into bed. And she had sent Lizzie a photo of him. He was posed skew-whiff at the corner of Leeson Street, his elbow at the postbox, an apple-cheeked lad, and Lizzie had written back, 'He's desperate skinny.' A real gent. His da's in the civil service, she'd told her, and he's going to college.

Yes, she had been right not to tell anyone. She was doing so well. Hopping from one exam to another, like a bird on a wire. And rendezvousing at six every evening. And then the wedding. Class! Nanny Wine turned into Nan McDonald. A nice professional name. Romantic. Made her think of claymores and warlike clans. She was on the road to fame.

'How's it going?' Maggie Slater yelled.
'Out for a walk.' It's well for some!
'Is Paddy beyant?'
Paddy Joe was not the full shilling. Liked to poke and pry.

He gave Nan the creeps, with his onion head and crooked smile. Supposing her own son . . . 'He's too good for the rest of them,' Maggie always said.

Maggie was a scrawny woman with dyed blonde hair and skin like cork. At night she put on high-heeled shoes and drank three delicate gins in Rogan's. She chain-smoked.

'No, only Fonsie,' Nan called back.

'You can't be at them,' Maggie said, stamping the fag underfoot.

Nan hurried on. She must get on. Get away.

In the distance the lake shone like the pelt of a seal. When at last she reached it she took off her shoes. Charles Henry Fordson. What a mouthful. A long way from Séan Wine the butcher's grandson. Plain Séan. No frills or attachments to the agnate side. Names are very important, her mother once told Nan. You grow into them. So he must have grown into a 'Charles' . . . The ghost of Séan?

She undressed and swam into the water.

'He's not coming here.'

'Then I'll go. To England. On my way back from Poland. Stop off. I could meet you at Heathrow.'

'Meet me? Who suggested I should go?'

'I'd need you there. We could have a holiday together. You're always saying we need a holiday.'

'A holiday! I was talking about the seaside. What sort of a holiday would that be with a thirty-year-old psychopath breathing down our necks?'

'Jim, you're being . . .'

'Unreasonable? A spoiled brat who's lost his mummy and daddy looking for a new crutch. Why did he wait all these years to look for you? Show me the letter again. Hmm. Parents killed in a car crash.' He threw it down. 'Do what you fucking well like, but count me out.' He took up his jacket. 'See you. I'm off to the pub.'

Nan sat on and stared at the door. What had she done? She should have torn up the letter and pretended it had never come. What was wrong with her? Had she no sense at all? Yet how could she have torn it up? The piece of paper, yes, but . . .

The sun was setting, a shock-red orb. Blinding. She watched a rook swoop down to peck around the grass for forgotten hen food. But . . .

Almost thirty to the day, he is!

Jesus!

The kitchen – their favourite room, with its nut-coloured walls and painted dresser, the Rayburn, Jim's pride, gleaming in the corner – had an unfriendly look on it this evening.

'No, we never fight,' she often told the neighbours. Even Ma Slater with her inquisitive nose.

But now?

Louis Wine had married a Catholic, Mary Halpin, who owned a general store in Tullyvon, County Cavan. They had four children: two sons and then, after a period of heart-scalding miscarriages, two daughters in quick succession. First Lizzie and then Nan.

When Lizzie was seven and Nan was five, Mary died. Of post-operative pneumonia. By this time Louis had expanded the shop into a grocers, vintners and victuallers, soon known as Wine's for wine and meat. 'The Jew man', they said, had fallen on his feet. Or, 'He's not a Jew for nothing.' Lizzie inherited her mother's fair complexion, a neat child with pale blue eyes that flew upwards when expecting a treat, while Nan was never out of trouble. For one she was always whistling. And a woman whistling, her aunt said, brought bad luck.

What had brought Louis Wine to this small Catholic village tucked away between two drumlins? Dark stories circulated. He'd been in trouble in the city. Over some shady deals perhaps. It was all conjecture. He didn't appear to follow his religion, while Mary brought up the children as good Catholics until, alas, she died.

After that things changed. The children no longer went to the chapel on Sundays and, oddest of all, young Nanny was said to be attending music lessons in Cavan town. At night Louis could be seen through the uncurtained window, sitting in his chair reading. Could it have been the Bible? If someone called, for a late purchase, candles or a bit of bacon, he would greet them cordially, unlock his shop and serve them, letting them off a penny or two if they were short.

Nanny adored her sister, believing that she was the acme of beauty and good manners. She enjoyed her piano lessons, it's true, but she found them so easy she couldn't take them seriously. Lizzie seemed superior in all the arts of young-ladyhood. Boys treated her with amazement, whereas they treated Nan with scant respect, grabbing at her when she got-off the bus at night, trying to pull her into corners, and on one occasion she nearly had her neck broken when a lad grabbed her hair and pulled her head around to kiss her slap on the lips. French-kissing, it was called, his buck teeth scalding her mouth.

Louis encouraged the two girls to take part in games of all kinds. Camogie in the winter and tennis in the summer. Little ladies, they were. Poor Mary Halpin would turn in her grave. When she was fifteen, Nan won the under-sixteens' singles in the Cavan tennis tournament.

The kitchen became eclipsed in twilight. The aluminium tea-pot on the dresser reflected the dying light. She had sat so long and stiffly on the deal chair that her thighs ached as she rose to go upstairs. But once in bed she couldn't sleep. When Jim eventually came up, he was noisily drunk.

As the hours passed and no sleep came, she rose and went down to her studio. She knew that now she must forget everything till after the concert was over. She opened the piano and laid her hands on the keys. Like a sick child whose brow is soothed by a loving touch, her body gradually uncoiled. She began on the Fauré, a piece so seemingly simple yet with every nuance a challenge. Little by little her playing took over. She played on through the night till dawn came, and then for several hours after, till her nervous energy was spent.

When Jim rose, grumpy, hungover, she attended to their breakfast while he watched her silently. When she offered some inanity, he didn't answer and, finishing his coffee, got up and wandered out. She watched him as he poked about, feeding the fowl and filling the buckets with water. In spite of herself she smiled. Ages ago she had offered to buy him a hose, which would save a lot of effort. But he'd refused, saying it was a waste of money. Secretly she knew it wasn't that. What he really enjoyed was stretching time.

But now she must work. Surely in time he'd come round. Or would he? Distracted, she returned to her room.

She extracted the Chopin 'Ballade' from a pile of music. If only the Poles would forget their hero! But imagine Salzburg, she supposed, without a Mozart. She knew she wasn't a Chopin pianist. Very few women can keep that necessary distance from his music. The very first time, years ago, when she had heard a recording of Horowitz playing a Chopin prelude, it had been an experience. Celebratory. Like being at an unexpected party. Maybe, also, the Slav character is needed. But, in spite of these misgivings, she soldiered on with the ballade, trying to give it her all.

Gradually her concentration flagged. Perhaps she was too tired. Was she finally being pushed into that tunnel she had managed to avoid all these years, her past thrown at her like a football? She banged out the last few chords of a passage. Tears began to blur the music sheets.

Charles Henry Fordson lying in his pram under the – what would it have been? – cedar tree. His face dappled, a wisp of wind shaking the leaves above. The oh so perfect mother picking him up when he whimpered, kissing him, his skin beneath her lips like indiarubber. Charles Henry Fordson, a lad tall for his age, riding his first bike, his father walking beside him, a grin on his face. Charles, now Charley, walking down the leafy lane to the local primary school.

She botched a bunch of semi-quavers in her left hand and automatically repeated them. Charley being shut in his room. Gated for a week. Caught reading filth. Mr Fordson saying, 'It's the bad blood.'

'You just want to put clean sheets on the past.' Jim, pretending to be immersed in the newspaper, refused to look at her. So. Nothing had changed.

She wanted to touch him but was afraid. Why couldn't she touch this skinny gentleman, forty-six years old, a little bit bald, with the look of a Wildean actor on him? Why couldn't she open his flies, like she sometimes did out of villainy when they were at some chore, and watch his eyes swivel with laughter?

'Jim, please . . .'

'I can see the headlines. Famous pianist finds long-lost son. God damn it. I won't be surrogate father to a stranger.' He slapped down the paper.

She got up and left the room. Yesterday, or was it the day before, he would have called after her, a bit of a joke, told her to let the dog out, not to bother to wash the dishes, and she would have gone back and pressed her pelvis against his knee, kissed the bald patch with a sly remark. But that was yesterday, or was it the day before? She had wanted to cry out, 'Jim! We are adult people.'

Jim sat at his desk. He was scorched by the fire of his anger. He didn't know why he was so angry, or what he was angry about. It seemed as though he could smell his rage and he was afraid of it. How dare she? How dare she keep all this to herself all these years?

A month back he'd been offered a residency in some college in downtown Sydney. How they had laughed at the notion. He remembered her hair brushing his cheek as they'd read the letter together. And he had taken a strand into his mouth. He loved chewing her hair, with its oily taste. Apparently a paper he'd read at the Archaeological Institute some years back had found its way into an Australian magazine and the college had been impressed. Together they had imagined the place, his colleagues with their long Aussie vowels expounding on abor-igine art. And how he'd have to explain the various theories of why the pre-Celts ever came to his own inhospitable isle. And all this without her. Without Nan! Jesus! Of course, he'd turned the offer down. But now was this the answer? A little time to think about it. Put it in perspective. But why hadn't she told him when first they'd met? Wouldn't they have dis-cussed it as time went on, speculated together about how her son would be and then, when finally he wanted to find her, they could share the responsibility together. Instead, she just throws out this information as though she'd left some dog in a kennel and wants to fetch it. How was he supposed to react? She might as well have banged him on the head with a mallet. But he was plagued by all those abstracts he'd ingested down the years. Loyalty. Loneliness. Dependence. Love? Was love an abstract? No. Love was a constant with which he and Nan had immunised themselves against the outside world. The result? Trust. The frangibility of trust. He ripped up some notes he'd been making and threw them in the bin. Hadn't that been enough for anyone in their middle years? Fuck it! How many could have boasted the same?

What about their neighbours, the Swanns? The Cob, the Pen and the two Cygnets? How would Nick react if Angela suddenly produced a grown-up child? Dr Nick Swann, with his cultured head of black hair, his two balding terriers, had become an amateur speliologist and was trying to persuade him to go to the Burren next week. At the moment he couldn't bring his mind round to exploring caves. Should he call on them? Maybe get some sympathetic advice. A change of scene might be all that was needed. From the habit of long association, he left a note: 'Gone to Swanns'.

It was ten past four, the time when Nan usually left off work and went for a walk. There was no sign of her. He tiptoed to the car and started it up. Thundering over the Swanns' cattle-grid, he observed the eldest Cygnet, an undergraduate at Trinity, going on to be a vet, exercising her show jumper in the paddock. He blew his horn in salute.

Every creature was asleep on this dreamy afternoon, the dogs stretched out flat as though dead. Ivy crept up the wall of the outside porch without a stir on it. He peered through the window and saw Angela bending over a plant. She struck him as looking like a browned teenager. Her hair in a single plait bounced between her shoulder blades. She was all brown, in fact. Her face and hands were weathered by sun and wind and she was wearing a brown T-shirt and striped brown and white shorts, beneath which her long legs culminated in a pair of open-toed sandals. He tapped on the glass. But as soon as he looked into the porch he knew he'd made a mistake. What had these super-normal people to do with his problem? When she saw him he attempted a smile.

'I heard the car,' she said. 'I thought it was Nick back early from surgery.' She held the door open for him. 'I'll make tea.

Bring out two chairs. Pity to be in, in this weather.'

'Your daughter is very energetic.'

'Patricia's off to Clifden tomorrow. For the horse fair.'

'It's a long way.'

Her small features, so unlike Nan's, caused a feeling of anguish to pass through him as she bent over to pour the tea. He had an urge to take her hand and pour out his troubles. But, as if on cue, the doctor drove up in his Volvo, grinding the gravel beneath his tyres.

Nick Swann's round head was all abeam. He threw off his doctoring jacket, loosened his tie and rolled up his sleeves. 'More like it,' he said.

Jim knew that his and Nan's childlessness was a matter of controversy in the neighbourhood. How people thought depended largely on their gender. Nan told him that Maggie was forever hinting that she felt sorry for them that had none to come after, followed up by how she'd never have managed without Fonsie. Onion-head, of course, was not mentioned in this category. The well-established Swanns, for all their breeding, often let the odd phrase drop. In fact, early on in their acquaintance, Nick had asked Jim if there was anything he'd care to talk about. Having a professional pianist as a wife – especially in the country – was, well, anomalous to happily wedded bliss.

'And how's Nan?' Angela broke the silence.

'Nan. Oh, Nan, yes. Nan's fine.'

'Jetting off soon?'

'Yes, next week. Poland.'

The elder Cygnet trotted past, causing dust to fly into the teacups.

'Patricia,' Angela shouted.

A right bitch, Jim thought, and was glad.

'I'll tan the hide of that one one day,' Nick said, pride oozing out of him.

'She'll keep us in our old age,' Angela smirked.

'There are no medical cards for animals,' Jim remarked.

The bold doctor was unshaken. 'And the heifers? All well?'

'It's not the calves. It's my dog, Shep. I have to lock him up. He was seen in McCarthy's, chasing sheep. Nan's very upset.'

'There's only one cure for that.'

Jim was sure their mouldy terriers wouldn't have the energy to worry sheep.

'Nan's soft on animals,' Angela commented.

Here we go, Jim said to himself. Childless woman soft on animals.

The Swanns were full of summer bonhomie, more interested in killing wasps than in Jim's dog problem. Dog problem! If only they . . . God, the lack of air, too, was getting him down. More than ever, he realised he shouldn't have come.

'I'd better go.'

Nick Swann woke up. 'What about the caves? Next Thursday OK?'

'Something's come up. I'll have to postpone the visit, if you don't mind.'

The doctor looked piqued but didn't comment. Jim rose, shaking the table so that tea spilt into the saucers. 'Thanks,' he said, with a grimace. 'A pint later perhaps?'

Reading Jim's note, Nan was annoyed. Should she follow him? Was he going to blurt out the problem to the neighbourhood, starting with the Swanns? If she followed him, she'd have to cut through Slater's fields and risk meeting Ma Slater again. Why had he sneaked off?

She set off down the road, past McGorman's cottage, newly whitewashed, with the old man sunning himself outside. 'How's it going?' he called.

She returned his salute. 'Mighty weather.'

'Mighty.'

He liked to chat. He had once driven a bus in Glasgow.

Nothing to it, he always said. But now he was too rickety, even for the bicycle. She listened for a moment to his oft-told tales before plodding on. But she had only gone a few yards when Jim pulled up beside her in the car. She climbed in and they turned back towards the house.

'So now,' Jim said.

'Now what? Did you bare your soul to the Swanns?'

'The conversation was desultory.'

'Good.'

They drove on in silence.

In the kitchen Nan said, 'I suppose you're full of tea and cake.'

'Just tea.'

'And the Pen? Tanned and fit?'

'Tanned.'

Nan made herself a single cup of tea with a tea bag. 'And what took you to the Swanns all of a sudden?'

'To tell Nick that I'm not going to the caves next week.'

'So what's wrong with the phone?'

'For fuck's sake, Nan, lay off the catechism, will you?'

'Sorry.' She went over to him to kiss the top of his head, but he pulled away.

'Nan, we've had a little time to think about things, so can we talk seriously about the dilemma?'

'Dilemma? Well, you begin.'

'I suppose you've written to tell them it's impossible? We need time. To make a decision.'

'I have not. We have to weigh all the pros and cons. And you have to calm down.'

'Me? It's you that's working yourself up into a maternal panic. A bit late in the day, wouldn't you think?'

'If you want to be spiteful there's no discussion.'

'All right, Nan. I'm sorry. You have to see him, I suppose. Otherwise you'll blame me for the rest of our lives together.' But as soon as he'd said this he felt his resentment flaring up again.

'There's a corner in my brain. You've been my life, Jim. All these years I've thought only of you, but from time to time that corner niggled.'

'I still don't understand why you didn't tell me years ago. Not in the beginning maybe but after we'd settled. Sure, we never had any secrets, did we? Well, you did obviously. And that hurts. I thought we always trusted each other.'

'I can't understand you. Was I supposed to blurt it out on our honeymoon? Or on our first date? If he hadn't decided to contact me, the secret would have remained locked up inside me for ever.'

'Blah blah blah!' He heard his voice rising.

'Everyone has secrets,' she shouted back. 'What about all the young ones you had the hots for on your travels?'

'That's completely different. I'm sure you often had the hots for loads of cellists or demonic Middle Europeans. Anyway, how long did you know this lout, this philandering lunatic who made you pregnant?'

'Once. In the biblical sense.'

'You expect me to believe that?' He got up abruptly and left the room.

Nan and Elsie were hiding from Miss Charity. 'Play that tune again, Nanny.' Nan went over to the ancient piano and started to pick out 'In the Mood'. Miss C marched in, a cloud of fury. 'You'll 'ave all the brats squalling. You, Elsie, upstairs with you and see to your kid. And you, Oirish, get your kid smartened up for them visitors. Coming to see it, they are. All posh, the adoption society says. Hupper-class, from what I 'ear. Don't know why, but the society said they wanted a good 'ome for your kid special.'

'Please, Miss, this is very sudden. Can I not have a few days to think about it?'

'A few days, she says, and me killing myself on your behalf.'

When Miss C had flounced out, Elsie put her arms around Nan.

'Nanny, you know you have to let him go. It's what you decided, remember?'

'I know, Elsie, I know. But you go through all those nine shitty months, ending up in this God-awful dump, with the likes of her shouting at you. I wish I'd never been born.'

'Come on, Nan. Remember all the laughs we've had in spite of the old bitch. Remember the time we snuck out to the caff and met them two dead-beats who bought us both a can of cider?'

'Oh, El, I'd die without you.'

'Lucky they didn't knock us up again!'

'Jesus, never. I'm never going near a man again s'long as I live.'

'That's all they do, them bastards. Knock you up and scarper. Can't see the dust once they've had you.'

'Did you like your feller, El?'

'Oh, a handsome bugger, all right. Promised to marry me and all, and buggered off the same day.'

'Like the dew on the rose.'

'Jesus, she's back!'

When hunger drove Jim back into the kitchen, without looking at Nan, he banged around as he made the supper.

'I had one friend in the hostel. A cockney girl, older than I was, but just as lost. In the hostel where I went to have the child. Séan. We called the bitch who ran the place Miss Charity.'

He had quickly made a spaghetti and was dishing it out on two plates. He sat down and forked some strands into his mouth.

'Why should this all come between us, Jim? We're the same couple as we were last week.'

'If you say so.'

'Her name was Elsie.' Nan banged her fork on the table. 'Jim, I loved her.'

'These people in your past! They've nothing to do with me.'

He wolfed down his food and got up. 'I'm meeting Nick in the pub.'

'Can I come? Please?'

'Feel free.'

As it was Friday the locals could not be expected to arrive till ten or half past. So when Jim and Nan went in the place was empty. The owner of the pub, Matt Rogan, was sitting with his back to the counter watching the nine o'clock news. They sat up at the bar and joined in the silent television-watching.

'Shocking.' Matt was commenting on the recent tragedy in Donegal, where two girls had been drowned while in the Gaeltacht. 'No supervision. That's the trouble.'

'Aye.'

'There's no need to get drowned,' Nan said.

Matt frowned at her.

Nick Swann came in and they all agreed once again that the drowning had been a terrible tragedy. 'Dreadful altogether.' Jim ordered a third pint.

'Not many sick this weather?' Matt queried.

'Francie McCarthy's mother has the shingles.'

'That's a terrible dose.'

'She must be a quare age.'

'Eighty-three.'

'Is she gone into the general?'

'Is Francie upset?' Nan asked.

'Ah, you know Francie.'

Jim's original plan to tap the doctor's brain for the pros and cons of a parent's meeting a long-lost child after so many years having fallen on its face, he now realised the evening might be as abortive as the afternoon had been. The doctor said he was expecting Patricia to drop in before closing time. Nan looked sideways at him. She and the eldest Cygnet did not see eye to eye.

Jim began to speculate about what it would be like if Nan's son were to walk in and be introduced all round. Soon divide the straw from the chaff.

Nan was wondering, would she recognise him? Would she hug him in front of everyone?

Jim felt as though his brain cells were dying, as though each one was being pricked with a needle. He could not gauge in his mind any more how Nick Swann would react if he told him about Nan's child. But it was now or never. Tell him he must. Man to man, or something like that. He fumbled for words. 'Nick, there's a problem I'd like to discuss.' But the latter was busy extending a fiver through a knot of shoulders pressed against each other at the bar. When he turned to Jim, he beamed a 'dear boy' beam, holding the purchased pints above his head. 'Shall we shelter in the other bar?' He made to brush through. Jim followed him out.

The back bar was a small hole of a place like an old-fashioned snug. Along each wall, onetime bus seats upholstered in torn rep sloped downwards. There was nowhere to put your pints.

'A problem?' Nick said.

So he had heard.

'What would you do if Angela told you she'd had a son thirty years ago by another man?' The words rushed out of him, as though he'd borrowed them from someone.

'But she hasn't.'

'Hypothetically, I mean.'

'I'd tell her to go and meet the bugger.'

'But wouldn't it upset you both?'

'Why should it?'

'Well, supposing you took a dislike to each other on sight?'

'I'd tell him to fuck off back where he came from. Why? Has Nan produced a child?'

They could hear the buzz of conversation in the other bar. The majority were divided on the issue as to whether O'Grady should have been sent off in last Sunday's GAA match, while Onion-head Slater was telling everyone what it had been like when he was an altar boy to Father Togher, the previous parish priest. And he could hear Nan talking to Martin O'Reilly, the electrical wizard.

'It's Nan's problem, is it not? I'd interfere as little as possible if I were you. Just be sympathetic till she sorts herself.' He shrugged. 'She seems OK.'

Jim wanted to scream, she's not, but instead glared into his pint. Eventually he said, 'These fuckers here would have a right laugh. I can just hear them: "The poor skinny craythur can't get it up. Childless blow-ins." How *am* I supposed to take it?'

Nick looked round at him. He was a big man, his arms bulging with healthy flesh. His face, like a squashed turnip, broke into crooked lines. 'A bit of a bummer, all right. She's going to meet him, I take it?'

'She has to, hasn't she?'

Yes, she had to.

Matt Rogan was turning on and off the lights. They bought two final whiskeys.

A little drunk, Nan had wondered in the pub whether they should now have a child. It still wasn't too late. But would it solve things? She fumbled around the kitchen. Every so often she opened her mouth to speak. A sort of craziness was on her. But she couldn't get the words out. Jim, on the other hand, seemed relaxed. He was reading the *Farmers' Journal*.

At last she began. 'Jim,' she said.

'Yes?'

'Oh, nothing.'

He shrugged, muttering, 'The price for heifers is down again,' and turned over a page. 'Should we get another?'

After she had gone to bed, he sat on. The paper fell to his knee. He was overcome with a need to put back the clock – not just to last week, but to all those long years ago when everything they did was filled with anticipation. When they touched each other, sparks flew. When Nan was away, he'd prowl the house, unable to work. And how he'd strain at the barriers in Dublin airport, terrified that she might have missed the plane. But before that there'd been this . . . this thing. He poured himself a measure of whiskey and swilled it round in the glass.

'We could still have a child,' she whispered as Jim levered himself into bed and turned his back on her.

He twisted round, startled, blood rushing to his crotch. The inside of her thighs, silky and wet. He could feel her arching her pelvis as his fingers fondled her pubic hair. Even if she didn't mean it, he felt his body tensing with excitement. 'Nan, Nan, Nan,' he muttered, licking round her ears, her chin, her mouth, and driving into her as if he'd waited all his life for this moment. The whole planet strained to meet him and they came simultaneously, like two trains crashing into a buffer.

When in bed later, Nick said to Angela, 'You'll never guess. Nan's had a baby.'

'So that's what was wrong with Jim earlier. Swivelling

round in his chair and talking arseways.'

'A thirty-year-old baby. A son.'

'That must have been painful.'

'He was a bit jarred, mind you. Which would account for his telling me. Apparently Nan doesn't know he's talked. So you say I never bring you news!'

'But why now? Why tell us after the skeleton has rotted in the cupboard?'

Nick explained as best he could, remembering Jim's need to talk, how upset he seemed. 'Hard to understand, mind you. But one can never gauge how stunned one might be under the circs.'

'Surprising, mind you,' Angela said cryptically. Nan's seeming self-assurance irked her. She laid down the book she was reading and shrugged herself under the bedclothes.

The swallows were flying low that morning. 'There'll be a break,' Nan said. 'It's a sure sign when they swoop down like that.' She had brought her cup of coffee outside and was sitting on an upturned log. Jim had trained honeysuckle over the near hedge and she smelled it sweet like almonds.

He dragged a chair out from the kitchen. Shep sat at their feet, a long rope attached to his collar. He barked when he heard the post van approaching.

'There'll be a break.' Jack said as he handed out the mail. 'That there will.'

There were no brown envelopes pre-franked from England. Jim tore the wrapper off the *Irish Times*. Now he had annoyed the doctor by postponing their trip to the Burren and he had blurted out his troubles in a drunken moment. How was he going to stop Nan getting to hear of his duplicity? He observed his calves, his pride and joy, nuzzling each other playfully. OK, they should have had children years ago. A pair of girls like the Cygnets. He should have insisted on it. He could have mustered up some sort of boring job in the Department of the Environment and been a civil servant like his father. But he didn't. A life unplanned had bowled along like a tram, Nan bringing in the money and he giving the odd lecture, the odd talk, writing the odd paper on some obscure findings. And now his playing the small farmer, typical blow-in, alternative, who can't even keep his dog from chasing sheep.

He looked over at her. She was sitting with one foot over a plump knee. A couple of years back they had decided they needed to get fit. Nan suggested yoga. So they had signed on with a neighbour, an alternative blow-in like themselves, who had started classes in her barn. But they kept missing appointments till they realised the futility of it. They had gone to the pub that night and laughed themselves silly. And then a few months ago they'd had some other daft plan. To attend the swimming pool in the town twice a week. Bright with enthusiasm, they'd kept this up a bit longer. Nan always worried about her weight. But again the repetition bored them and they'd given up.

Gingerly he laid his hand on her knee. 'Nan,' he began. She turned her huge eyes on him but no words came. She got up and ran into the house.

Her fingers rested on the ivory keys. She sat like that, a Pre-Raphaelite position yet so different from those languid English women who posed for Burne-Jones or Rossetti. A stocky figure in shorts and sleeveless vest, with her hair pinned up in a peak, her forearms muscled like a jockey's, she had that tomboy look Jim delighted in.

OK, they should have had children long ago, two sons like whom? Hardly Fonsie and Onion-head. She racked her brain for friends with grown-up sons. Yes. She could have chucked her career – or put it on hold at least – let Jim be whatever, the bread-earner like all their acquaintances in Dublin – very respectable, respected. Yes, she should have insisted – but it was she who had refused in the first place. They'd have been poor, scraped along, saved to send the children to the best schools, to college, to pay for their detox when they got caught up in the drug culture. She could have played honky-tonk in a bar, like so many failed pianists, for extra pocket money. And now she could botch her concert. And her so-called career could end as abruptly as the heatwave was about to end in the next few hours. To the west, beyond her window, clouds gathered. As in the morning, swallows streaked past her window, a distant pheasant coughed, rooks disbanded in the chestnut tree and her pelvis contracted in memory of the previous night. A desperate ploy on her part, what had she been thinking of? Still. It was the best thing that had happened for many a day. She started on the sonatas.

'I'm thinking of cancelling the concert. Weighed against travel expenses, it's worthless.'

'I thought you loved Poland.'

'I'm not ready for it. Even if it is in a tiny hall, I have to keep up my reputation.'

'What about my reputation? I'll be the laughing stock of the parish.'

'We're living in the 1990s, Jim. What's your reputation to do with it? You didn't father the child and abandon it. Leave me to sort things out till I can come back and everything will be as it was a week ago.'

'Nan, when I married you, you were an intelligent woman. How can things ever be the same? You. Yes, you will be different.'

They were back down that blocked drain again. Jim, as usual fiddling with the newspaper, got up and suggested she might clear up the mess.

'Mind your metaphors,' Nan snapped. And as he was

leaving the room she shouted, 'All right. I'll go to Poland. Chance the concert and call into the English village on my way home. He won't like the look of me anyway. I'll be so different from his adoptive parents. He'll expect somebody languid and stick-like in a brown cardigan over a flowered dress, with brown, slightly greying hair pulled back in a bun ... '

He was out the door as her speech dried up.

But she couldn't stop wondering how her son would look. She had a vision of his being like her father, Louis Wine. That remote, studious man who looked after his shop, made enough money to feed, clothe and educate his children and whom she had betrayed by leaving him alone when the other fledglings had flown the nest. Yes, it was she who was to look after him in his old age. To play in local halls, accompanying the singers who visited the town from time to time. Who would have given music lessons to the young ladies of the parish, and perhaps married eventually the solicitor's son, Gavin O'Reilly, and set themselves up in the town.

She imagined walking towards this man, her son, down an immaculate village street, a street with Elizabethan houses leaning askew, a village with curiosity shops and tea rooms, a tall pub called the Horse and Hound, a bank and a demure supermarket. She would have to introduce herself because he wouldn't recognise her. All this in her head and yet she hadn't even answered the letter. She shut the lid of the piano and began to write.

'You do realise that some of those English villages have no pubs.'

'That's impossible.'

'They are a primitive race. Nan, you don't realise.'

'But he has Irish blood. Surely he wouldn't live in a village without a pub.' Was she really having this conversation?

Her father, Louis Wine, had never been a drinker. He might take a bottle of stout, or a small whiskey on a cold day or at a wake. Strange. She never thought of his Jewishness until lately. And yet when his sisters had come to his funeral the hearse had gone to Dublin and the service had been held in the small Jewish synagogue in Adelaide Road. She and her brothers and sister had felt embarrassed when her brothers had been handed the yarmulkas to put on their heads. The four siblings had come from different parts of Ireland when they heard the news. Her two brothers from Limerick, where they had set up as accountants, and her sister from Westmeath, where she was married to a farmer.

Aunt Aggie, their mother's sister, had telephoned them that morning in February. An icy wind had cut into her as she went out into Westland Row, having just finished a lesson in the Academy, and she had gone back to her digs after arranging to meet Jim in the café opposite Dwyer's pub.

'Do you remember the day I met you in that café – what's this its name was? – opposite Dwyer's, and I told you I had to rush home because my father had had a stroke? When I got to Tullyvon he was in a coma. It was terrible to see him like that. Such a strong man. We all expected him to live for another twenty years.'

'You never spoke of your father after that.'

'I was consumed with guilt. I should have stayed at home to look after him. And married Gavin O'Reilly.'

'Oh, no! Now the shit is hitting the fan. So this O'Reilly character is the father of that English person!'

'Dear God, no.' Nan nearly laughed. 'And don't keep

harping on his Englishness.'

'I have refrained from asking this creature's parentage, but you might as well tell us now. Not that I care who the fucker was.' Jim took a swipe at a fly with his newspaper.

'He was my partner in the mixed doubles.'

'And his name?'

Nan had never told anyone the father's name. Either the few people in whom she had confided refrained from asking or she had pretended she didn't know. Poor Elsie in the hostel even, with whom she had been so close, had asked her and she just said 'a bloke I met at a party.'

'And did you fancy him?' Elsie asked.

'He was gorgeous, like a Roman god. His hair curling down the back of his neck. A student from Dublin.'

'Cor. Wish I got one like that. I'd a hung on to him.'

'Thought you liked your feller?'

'Yeah. S'pose I did, the bastard.'

'But it was just the once. I never told him. He never knew.'

'His name?'

'There's no point in dragging that up. Just forget it. Think of it as the Immaculate Conception.'

'Always flippant. So he has become famous, has he? Is he a politician, the Taoiseach? No point in hiding anything any more.'

'It's not important, Jim. It's all so long ago.'

'Well, if I do have to meet this person, I'd like to know at least who his father was.'

'That's ridiculous. If you meet one of your colleagues, do you not deign to speak to them unless you know their parentage?'

Jim got up. There was no point in talking to Nan in this

mood and he said as much when he left the room.

She had never longed, had no photos of him in the cradle. Only the mist of a memory of a howling infant and her feeling of lightness when he was taken away.

And now she could see him. Actually see him.

Meet that baby, grown up. An individual.

The son of the one who had perpetuated that seed innocently garnered in that hotel after the tennis tournament. Their first kiss in the pavilion. While sheltering from the rain.

What a conception!

She smiled in the dark, once again unable to sleep.

At six she rose and roamed the house. She should use the time to practise, but she couldn't bring herself to go near the piano. She could hear Jim's snores, like the distant *phut* of a motorbike. She looked out at the dawn. A bird fluttered. A twig fell. All so pervasive. So soft.

She felt a feverish glow on her. I *must* see him, she muttered. I have nothing to lose. This person cannot harm me, after all.

The dawn widened. The sun rose. There were noises. Jim was up. As she entered the kitchen, she said, 'I can't sleep.'

He didn't look at her. His glances, like his words, had changed. He didn't talk like he used to before the news. The news that had come in an unfranked brown envelope.

He stood by the singing kettle, reading yesterday's paper.

'People with high cheekbones age well,' he remarked.

'Fuck you. What do you care if I'm at breaking point?'

'I was only talking about Elizabeth Taylor. Did you know her real name was Marion Morrison? And you've got high cheekbones, so that proves it.'

'Please, Jim, I'm worried sick.'

And when he said, 'I know,' she burst into tears. Instead of wanting to hug her, Jim wanted to laugh. 'Nan,' he said, through suppressed giggles, 'Nan, for fuck's sake go back to bed. I'll call you at half ten.'

He looked up the time of the lecture. If she drove him to the station he could catch the one thirty. He watched her trying to gulp back her sobs. He began telling her of his plans for the day, how important it was for him to hear the Zirkov lecture, how the man rarely visited Ireland, when she shouted at him, 'Don't give me all that academic shit.' She staggered out into the morning warmth. Jim recoiled. Was his increasing lack of interest in his career really so obvious? That game they played – of the eternal present, the now – had it all been make-believe? But, God damn it, I love the bitch. Am I supposed to share her now? With a stranger? Someone full of bitterness, perhaps, who would weave his way into her heart? He sat stiffly on the edge of his chair. Why couldn't this sameness continue? Like jogging along in an ass and cart. Bumpy but secure ... Was the whole parish laughing at him? Did Nick Swann think him a charlatan? Nick Swann, with his continent of friendly flesh, had sewn up his life in a parcel of respectability. Just then he felt he'd love to tear the strings apart and find there a seed of dirt, or even a seed of doubt, come to that.

He watched his wife on her hunkers stroking Shep. He suspected she was still weeping. She was nuzzling the dog's ears and Shep responded by licking her salty face.

She rose and, taking Shep on his lead, walked through the yellowing grass. Two hens followed her, expecting their breakfast. She shooed them away. She crossed the fence into Slater's meadow. The first cuttings of the silage were rolled into their plastic containers. She prayed that Maggie wouldn't emerge. She imagined herself introducing her son, Charles Henry Fordson. 'This is my son!' 'What? I didn't know ye had any children. Isn't he a fine man. Has he been away?' And then the whole townland having a gawk at her, as if she was a billboard advertising contraceptives.

Should she go to see Nick Swann in his surgery? He'd be there now, she reckoned, and she'd have time if she doubled back on to the road and walked down to the village. She could ask him his doctorly advise. God knows he must be used to the most appalling confessions. Spots on the willy, supurating vaginas. A mere baby. Didn't Mary's daughter take the boat only last week?

Dr Swann had two partners, one of whom was slow to give out prescriptions and everyone avoided. Swann's manner had that mixture of good-natured banter and seriousness that people trusted.

'Well, Nan?' he said, giving her his perfected keen glance.

'Physically well but ... I need your advice. What would you say if Angela confessed to you that she'd had a child before she met you and that he had suddenly turned up? That he had traced his parentage?'

Nick felt as if he were about to make the same bed twice. He said, 'I can't imagine it. If Angela had a child adopted she'd have told me years ago.'

'That's the whole point. I didn't tell Jim in the beginning and then it was too late. Don't forget, having an illegitimate child in those days was worse than AIDS today. It didn't matter how many guys you slept with so long as you didn't get caught. But a baby! Curtains to a relationship. Besides, I was a serious pianist. I knew I could make my career that way.'

'You are telling me, Nan, that you had a child before you met Jim and had it adopted?'

'Yes. That in itself is bad enough, but now I've had a letter to say he has tracked me down and wants to meet me.'

Nick shifted. 'So Jim is upset? And you don't know what to do?'

'Upset! He's acting pig obstinate. Threatening to piss off.'

For the first time in their acquaintance, he saw Nan in a different light. A woman with so much self-assurance but with whom he had little in common had come to him for help. He pushed back his chair. 'What you're doing at the moment is worrying about Jim and not thinking rationally about your own reactions. Do you really want to see your son?'

'Yes.'

'Then you must go. You have no choice. I must say, if I were Jim I'd be curious to see a son of my wife's I hadn't met. Seems he's making a meal out of it.'

Nan hadn't expected this. Men usually stick together, don't they?

'But then you've already got children. So it's different.'

Aha, Nick thought, as he pared a pencil into a fine point.

Nan gazed at the wallpaper especially put there to amuse toddlers, Walt Disney themes dripping like dog-ears at the corners, and thought, fuck, I hate kids.

'It's a bad time for you, just as you are approaching the change.'

Now he was inferring 'woman's trouble', like every other male omadhan she'd ever met.

'I don't think that's worthy of you, Nick. What about Jim and his menopause?'

She knew she'd have to end the interview before she said anything she'd regret. Fuck him, anyway, and his tanned wife, his healthy successful brats. So the whole situation hinged on her and Jim's original decision never to have children. What's done is done. She realised, then, she had no intention of having a menopause child who would probably turn out a Down's. In spite of what she'd said in that moment of sexual abandon. What had she been up to?

'You are off soon, aren't you?'

'Oh, it's all airports and musty hotel rooms. If I'm lucky the flight allows me a day off to roam. I love Poland . . .'

Why had she come? She knew the gap between them was too wide for any real rapport. He could only mouth his doctorish platitudes. She had made him nervous. He probably wanted to get rid of her. Most likely he thought they were making a mountain out of a molehill, but when she said as much he said, 'Some molehill.'

'So you think it's a serious matter?'

'Very. Dangerous. I really wouldn't like to be in either of your shoes.'

She explained a little about his circumstances, that his parents had both been killed recently. And the doctor did a lot of hmming.

'All I can say, Nan, is take care. Be very cautious when you meet him. Don't make any promises.'

Was he thinking mostly about Jim now, she wondered.

'Don't ask him here until you're absolutely sure what you're doing. Remember Jocasta!'

Surprised at the reference, she wondered were they now all jumping on the Oedipal wagon, as the doctor muttered on, 'There's nothing much you can do at the moment. Perhaps make a fuss of your husband.'

She left him there, tapping his teeth with his pencil, thinking, sententious bollocks! What a waste of time!

Once home, she skirted Jim's study and went to the piano. She tried to distil some hope into her fingers, but she played mechanically, note-perfect, without an iota of feeling.

Jim packed his overnight bag, put on a clean shirt and called Nan, 'Can you leave me down? Sorry to interrupt.'

In the car they kept silent.

With a feeling of relief, he watched the dried-up midlands flashing past his window. The few lakes they passed had turned into puddles. This heatwave was getting cumbersome, although droughts in Ireland were seldom serious. The grass still grew, the animals ate and drank – more work for the farmers, watering the beasts, of course – something to complain about. He watched a child in his shirtsleeves drive a tractor over a hillock. It bucked like a horse on the descent. At Maynooth a rake of students piled in and he had to shift his papers to make room on his seat. A glossy-haired lassie stuffed herself in beside him. She was half pretty, tanned like the rest of the Irish population and clearly gone on the boy opposite. They talked about exams and he gathered they were both studying computer science.

He bought another cup of Iarnrod Eireann coffee and a steam-rolled sandwich, making a jocular remark about the catering. The student looked at him – who did he think he was, the old fart? You'd be surprised, he silently answered their unspoken thoughts. When I was your age ... forty, well fifty, well fifty-year-olds had their unique attractions. Depending on the gender, of course. He remembered Nan going on *ad nauseam* about her tutor, who, to him, seemed senile. This is no country for old men, he quoted to himself, and thought about Sydney. Ireland is too fucking youth-orientated. You couldn't get into a pub on the south side of Dublin any more without being jostled by unmannerly louts and loutesses. And where did they get their money? From their thieving parents, he supposed – the tax-dodging Dublin 4 brigade. Not from working in a chemist's shop for three pounds a week at the bottom of Lesson Street, for sure.

The two were smiling at each other conspiratorially, as if they'd both just got up out of bed – the same bed. No tossing off in the bicycle shed these days, with condom machines in every cranny of the college. An old man with bitter thoughts, he turned his attention back to the canal, now ecologically clean, a purple ribbon, no prams or Volkswagens like in the old days. Only an occasional swan – which reminded him – God, he hoped the Cob hadn't blathered to anyone about his confession. The thought would nearly force him to join the AA. Away from home now, the fog of insecurity seemed to have lifted. His spirits rose.

What was he worried about anyway? Supposing Nan did get herself entangled with this man. There was always Sydney. Australia's huge, full of widows and divorcées with neatly grown-up children. Not to mention raunchy little students fascinated by his Irish consonants and vowels.

Alighting at Connolly, he took a taxi to South William Street and ensconced himself in a bar. It was too early for the mob. He ordered a pint and snuggled into a corner.

The lecture wasn't till seven, so he planned a nice Indian meal, a stroll around the green and after the lecture he assumed he and Zirkov would take off to the Shelbourne. Hopefully some young female sycophants would be in tow and liquor would flow. Greatly cheered, he downed a second pint. But you never knew with Middle Europeans nowadays. Since the fall of Communism, they had become very dull – there was no need to be subversive any more. An open society led to all kinds of lacklustre ideas.

'You didn't stay long.' They were at their snack lunch the following day. 'Was your man interesting?'

'No.'

'Wasn't it worth it then?'

'Dublin is trying too hard. Everyone in mad extremes. As if they are being paid to pose for vodka and Guinness ads. And the price of drink!'

'I have a confession to make.'

'Have you found any more children?'

'I went to see Nick Swann to get advice.'

'Did he say ... What did he say?' Jim tried hard to breathe evenly.

'He took the problem seriously.'

'He didn't say anything else? Did he say anything about me?'

'Just to treat you more sympathetically. Which I am

going to do now. He was tedious about my hormones,' she added.

Jim let out a deep sigh.

After a pause, she said, 'You seem to be very bitter.'

'About what?'

'Oh, everything. Having married a professional woman. Never having had kids, or a normal nine-to-five life. Dinner on the table. Bijou dinner parties, lace cloths and candlelight. Especially now that this has all come up.'

'Jesus, what sort of crap have you been reading?'

'Also having a mistress. All those kinds of people have mistresses, penthouse flats in the city.'

'Jesus, I never wanted children. Isn't it always women who want children?'

'But Swann seems to think it's the nub of the problem. Why you're afraid to met my son.'

'Did he say that to you?'

'No, but his remark about my hormones made me think that's what he meant.'

Jim didn't want to think about Nan's hormones just then, but he couldn't help remembering the rush of adrenaline they'd both experienced the last time they'd made love. But it made no sense.

He couldn't gather his thoughts. His trip to Dublin had been a waste of time. All he wanted was to get back into his comfortable mould.

'Did you feed the calves?'

'And the hens.' Nan wanted to get up and hug Jim but was afraid of being rebuffed. 'One of them is broody. Better get a setting from Angela. Do you think the Swann's eggs are fertile?'

They both looked at each other, little dribbles of laughter breaking open their faces.

'I'm sure the doctor's had the snip.'

That afternoon Nan practised with a semblance of authority. Something, if not everything, had changed for the better. Had his day away from her brought him a glimmer of understanding? His trip had upset him. She wondered, would he tell her why? Perhaps he had hoped some bimbo would share his hotel bed and the arrangement had fallen through. He loved sniffing around young women, she knew. Such a skinny yoke, like an elderly boy! Charm the birds off the trees, he could, with his daft laughter, his wayward remarks. The bollocks! She still felt jealous when he looked sideways at that Greta one in the pub. Or even Angela. She often wondered, did he stray into foreign beds at all? God knows, he had plenty of opportunity while she went on her travels. The thought caused her left hand to miss a grace note. All these Oedipus/Jocasta hints were getting on her nerves. She was curious, simply curious to see her son. She felt no umbilical pull, as they all seemed to think. But they wouldn't believe her. What was it Jim had said at first, all that soak it in motherhood bit? And the doctor and his fucking hormones. Her playing got worse as her thoughts fell back into the old tracks. She must put all that behind her till after the concert. Think of more important things, such as what she should wear. The black and gold or the black and gold? Or the bottle green which off set her brown eyes? My beautiful brown eyes, she said, as she stared into the polished wood of her Bechstein. Jim looked drawn and pale, probably has a fierce hangover, she thought, as she finally shut the lid.

He was at a loose end. The heifers were fed and watered. Nan always forgot to water them, as if they were camels, and when he'd brought them up the buckets they had drunk with great gulping sounds. What if he'd stayed away another few days?

Imagine coming home to four dead calves! He realised suddenly that this was what he really loved doing. Pottering about with his animals, playing the squire and small farmer. Fuck speliology, palaeontology and all other ologies. And there was Nick Swann wanting to drag him off on some new spurious hunt for the past. Why couldn't he just stick to doctoring, which he must be good at?

Seriously, had he ever really wanted children? He tried to dig into his past emotions on the subject. Nan was the boss and that suited him. All those years when they'd lived in Dublin, he had worked to remind himself of his chosen career – lectured, researched and written a decent sort of thin book on Bronze Age cairns with special emphasis on the use of metals and stones for ornaments or religious artefacts such as jasper, steatite and sea shells. He had accompanied Nan on her tours. He and an undergraduate had combed Ireland for any undiscovered passage tombs or dolmens. They had climbed up to Loughcrew and were surprised at the lack of interest it garnered when they enthused about it later. He remembered turning down a trip to Egypt because he was afraid Nan would run off with someone else if he was away for long. Then ... But, Jesus, his anxieties came flooding back. What had she been doing? Who had she been with, who had fathered this child? He had never known jealousy, but suddenly he felt that serpentine monster curling round his chest. What about that electrical fucker? Did she really fancy him? As he cleaned the henhouse, forking out the droppings on to a barrow, and went to fetch fresh sawdust, he found new anxieties attacking the horizon of his mind. What would happen if he really went away? As he wheeled the barrow to the compost heap, he smelled the sweet smell of hen shit, thinking, I must cut the grass. Yes, tomorrow I will cut the grass ...

The sun was well into the west. He skirted his own field and, instead of taking the route Nan always took, turned right into Gilsenan's and edged along the headland of a meadow recently cut. The Gilsenans were an eccentric lot. There had been three brothers but one of them had died mysteriously. He had been found in a ditch, allegedly having lost his way home after a feed of drink in Lawlor's. Lawlor's was 'the other pub', and the adherents of each pub boycotted the other one. Rogan's catered for the adjacent farmers, but there were those who'd walk or drive the extra two miles to avoid it. Old feuds, or some recent insult in one or other of the pubs, caused the social rift. And they would vow that they would never be seen again in whichever pub they avoided. With these thoughts in mind, Jim had a notion he'd drop into Lawlor's. As a blow-in he had not made any lasting decisions about either of them. They where both dirty, in the winter freezing – Lawlor's was marginally warmer than Rogan's, and Lawlor had more of a personality than Matt Rogan. The former, with his criminal eyes, had a charm of his own. Nan liked him for his flirty innuendoes, whereas Matt Rogan made blank statements about every mortal thing mostly to do with money.

When he entered the place it was as dark as night. Nick Swann, he thought, should come here more often to satisfy his trogloditic needs.

'Mighty weather,' Jack Lawlor said as he pulled a pint.

'There was supposed to be a break,' Jim said.

Jack looked through his eyelids at him as though he'd made a pass. 'Divil a break.'

Jack came back out from behind the bar to where he had been when Jim came in to a seat in front of the telly. The Sunday drinkers had all been turfed out around three in various stages of alcoholic stupor, staggering into the blistering heat to go home to the bacon, spuds and cabbage, and Jack had settled down to eat his own dinner of sirloin steak, carrots, peas and onions. He ate well and the remains on his plate were congealing beside Jim on the counter. While he was enjoying the first pint, Pat Mullen barged in.

'A pint of stout.'

'You've had enough,' Jack said, without getting up.

Pat swayed on his heels. 'A pint of stout.'

No move from Jack.

'I'd appreciate it,' Pat said, 'if you'd give me a pint of stout.' Swaying backwards he had to latch on to the bar stool to keep himself from falling. 'It's nice to be nice,' he said, looking at Jim as though he'd just seen him. 'It's nice to be a bollocks.'

Jack continued to look at the telly.

Pat extended his hand to Jim and Jim shook it. 'It's nice to be a bollocks.'

Pat lived alone, an orphan bachelor of forty-five. He had a few acres and a herd of mixed cattle. Jim had sympathy for him, suspecting that he didn't eat enough, and on Christmas Day he and Nan brought him down a plate of turkey and ham. They shook hands for the third time and grew silent. Jim drank, Jack watched the box and Pat stood a little away from the counter, confused by the recalcitrant world. He had never been known to sit, as though he could only trust the un- dulations of the floor, like a sea creature who's just discovered land. His head hung into his chest. His young feminine features showed surprise.

After his third pint Jim got up and wished them well, stroll- ing into the setting sun. The horizon was tinged with purple and he experienced a twist in the gut. If only things could con- tinue thus. If only he could now return home to the place he loved and find Nan, humorous, caustic and, yes, beautiful Nan in her usual place in the kitchen, reading the paper, laughing over the latest political scandals. The way she spread the paper right out on the table as if it were a map! They used to have so many things in common. But, Jesus, with this fucker lurking round the corner ... The three pints, which at first had lifted his spirits, were now making him maudlin. His shirt caught on a strand of barbed wire as he crossed into his field. 'Fuck it,' he shouted. Fuck it anyway. He had bruised his elbow on a stone.

Nan wasn't in her usual post-walk place. The kitchen was empty and, since she had insisted on removing the fly paper, the insects buzzed and swarmed everywhere. He picked up the *Irish Times* and swatted the ceiling and the walls. Where the fuck was she? He called round the house with no result. He'd a mind to go out again, this time to Rogan's, and get blocked out of his head. If he didn't cook the supper, she'd have a disgruntled look on her when he returned. For the first time ever he felt like throwing everything in, packing his bags and walking out the house. What good was he anyway? An adjunct to a professional pianist! A house-husband. To hell with it. All that sentimental twaddle he'd indulged in earlier! *Finita la comedia!*

So she had crawled to Swann – and the doctor, a decent man, had not betrayed his confidence. Doctors have their Hippocratic oath to protect themselves from infidelities, he assumed, as he unhooked his jacket from a nail on the back door.

The evening air was still warm, the swallows once more high above the trees. Nan had taken the car, so he'd have to walk to Rogan's, sod it. The road was empty of human or vehicle and he began thinking about gin and tonics, but as he rounded the corner he met a herd of cattle being followed by Onion-head Slater on his tractor. He stepped aside, trying not to look the bull in the eye. He had no confidence in the saying that bulls won't chase you if there are cows around. He prepared himself to jump the ditch if necessary. He saluted Slater half-heartedly as the animals trotted past, the cow's udders swaying from side to side like shopping bags. Nan, although always worrying about her weight, still had the figure of a twenty-year-old. None of your sagging-breasted matrons of hereabouts. Apart from Angela Swann, whose breasts were like two fried eggs, the mammalian average for the over-forties must be pretty high. Men are supposed to like enormous breasts, but he must be an exception. He seemed to go for neatly rounded appurtenances of the half-grapefruit variety. And here came Gilsenan senior. Raphael Gilsenan had the suspicious walk of one who carried a load of guilt. Had he or had he not been responsible for his younger brother's death? They were a well-got crowd, reputedly mean, tight as a baby's arse if it came to helping out a neighbour. It would stand to reason that he wouldn't share his farm three ways when his old man died. His father was in his dotage. Late at night in Rogan's he'd burst into a moist-eyed:

> Love is teasing and love is easing
> And love's a pleasure when first it's new.
> But when you grow older, love grows colder
> And fades away like the morning dew.

Whereupon Raphael would drive him home

He wondered what Raphael was doing on his feet at this hour. Normally he rode in his smart four-wheel drive, his massive shoulders and square head squashed down in the driver's seat. Bit of a hunch on him, all right. Did he wonder who was walking behind him late at night when he went into the byre, his lantern swinging?

And fuck it. There, outside the pub, was their car.

Nan, having wondered about Jim's absence for over two hours, assumed – wrongly – that he must be in Rogan's. Having made herself two slices of toasted cheese, she decided to follow him.

Martin, the electrician, about whom she indeed had sexual fantasies, was there already. Having established the fact that he was enjoying the heat, she curled herself up at the bar beside him. With Martin, she usually embarked on a complicated conversation about cars. In his spare time he was handy with carburettors and water pumps. She needed a bit of space, to try to get things into perspective.

'Hubby away?' Martin smiled fully into her face.

She wanted to tell him he had the sexiest eyes in the parish but instead said, 'No, he's stravaguing, gone missing.'

'I wouldn't say that'd be very far.'

She searched for innuendo but found none. Could she lure him into bed if Jim really did leave her? But then, would she want to? He did have a wife, of course, but she was rumoured to be having it off with Barney Smith, a Protestant farmer and general entrepreneur who lived the other side of Clogher. He was teaching her to water-ski in the long evenings on Lough Melden, a man who liked his lassies fair and sporty as he showed off his skill with his new motor boat.

They were both laughing when Jim walked in. Nan straightened her face as he sat down beside her.

'You came the long way round.'

'I was home and you weren't there. I've been through five townlands at least since I saw you.'

'I see,' she said, knowing he must have been in Lawlor's, a name that could not be spoken aloud in Matt's hearing. 'A pint of stout,' she called.

'Hi, Martin,' to the latter's, 'Hi, Jim,' and Nan sat glumly between them, the spell broken.

'If you're not hungry, I am.' Jim kicked over the rack of vegetables; carrots, turnips, and garlic went flying. 'If you weren't in love with that ebony beast,' he shouted, kneeling on the tiles, 'you'd have a nice dinner waiting for me when I came home.'

'Don't call my piano a beast and don't give me that shit about housewifeliness.'

He wanted to break all the rules, beat the face off her. 'You're so sure of yourself. You think I'm a wimp to be trodden on like an old rug. A frayed rug at that.'

'What's the matter with you? Get up off the floor, for fuck's sake.'

She really wanted to say, 'You're drunk. You're just a bad drunk. Just ease up on the booze and you might see sense.' But she was torn. The threat of her son seemed to be destroying his self-esteem. Something she had hoped never to see. But there were only three days before she'd be flying to Warsaw and she mustn't go down that road. The 'being impatient with Jim' road. Blocked many, many years ago.

'I'm sorry I lost my rag.' She put a hand on his shoulder.

'Cat's miaow.'

They ate silently till Jim barked out, 'So, before you go, are you going to tell me or are you not?'

'Tell you what?'

'The father's name and how and what.'

'I told you, there's no point. And as for how and when, it was raining and he had already tried to kiss me where you change your shoes. You see, I had no partner in the mixed doubles and we had been chatting while we looked out at the rain. Little peardrops bouncing on the edge of the pavilion.'

'You mean you were fucking like rabbits in the pouring rain.'

'I said we were standing where you change you shoes.'

'I'm not asking for the gory details, I just want to know who to expect home next week. Am I to expect some broken-hearted mother with her boobs hanging loose?'

Nan turned her back on him. 'You're no different from what you'd have been thirty years ago. Wise up, Jim, for fuck's sake. Or will I cancel the meeting? Forget I'd ever got the letter? Tell him it's too late?' She swivelled round on him. 'Is that what you want?'

'But you won't do that.'

'Then can we not come to terms with it rationally?'

'There is no rational. It's too late for logic.'

'Are you not coming to see me off?'

'Have I any choice? I have to drive you to the airport, haven't I?'

The weather had finally broken the previous day. Lightning had forked through the trees. Then came the downpour. Rods of rain clattered on the tin roof of the shed. The chickens rushed for cover, bodies bent into the ground; the heifers huddled at the gate, bemused teenagers. And today there was a steady drizzle with a chill wind. 'It's like winter,' the postman said.

Nan ran around like a maenad, while Jim insisted on reading the paper. She felt tearful and lost. Normally he would have been finding things for her, seeing she'd got her passport, foreign currency, all the last-minute trivia. 'Do you mind?' she shouted as she fell over him for the tenth time.

He shrugged. His mouth a bland rictus. And he recrossed his legs, turning over a page.

She had to fly from Knock, via London, to Warsaw. 'I hate this. I hate flying. I hate you.'

Jim laughed, overtaking a car on a corner.

'Jesus.'

'Yes, Jesus,' he said, laughing some more.

Heavy gusts of rain were sweeping across the runway. With her handbag sliding off her shoulder, Nan humped her suitcase across the car park, the rain running into the back of her collar, her hair streeling round her face. What a bastard, what a fucking bastard, she fumed, as she arrived at the check-in, her wits astray, fumbling in her handbag for the ticket.

Jim turned the car without looking back and drove slowly

from the building, but as soon as he was out of sight he slowed
to a halt and gazed ahead for a long time. His stomach was
coiled in a knot. He tried to straighten his body, taking deep
breaths, lifting his arms above his head. He got out of the car
and attempted to fart, but, afraid he might shit his pants, got
back in and turned for home. He heard the aircraft revving up
and in spite of himself he felt that familiar contraction of fear in
his pelvis. 'What do I care? What do I care if the fucking plane
crashes? If it falls out of the air in a ball of fire.' But he couldn't
stop himself from watching through the window to see it was
safely airborne.

They hadn't lit a fire that summer, so he made an attempt to
rake the ashes from the Rayburn and tidy up generally.
Shagging chaos, that's what she leaves, shagging chaos in her
wake. She's right, too, this thirty-year-old infant won't want
to see her as she is. You'd have to scratch through the globe to
find a less maternal woman than Nan.

Cheered by this thought, he decided to go to Rogan's for a
pint. Should he ring Nick to see if he was thirsty? Maybe from
the pub.

'That's a hardy one,' Matt said.

'A bit of a change all right. And a half-one,' he added.

She'd be in Heathrow by now, trundling her suitcase from
one end of the airport to the other. He downed his pint and
ordered another.

'Nan not coming down?'

'She's gone.'

Matt raised his eyebrows and turned back to the telly.

After a while he managed to lure Nick to the pub. 'She's
gone,' he said, by way of greeting as Nick shuffled himself on
to a bar stool.

Nick could see that Jim was half cut. 'Angela's on her way.
The girls have gone to town. Perhaps you should talk to her.'

Jim's reaction to Nan's news had been peculiar. He wondered, for the first time seriously, how he would feel if he was suddenly faced with a ready-made son. 'I wouldn't like to be in your boots,' he said in an attempt at sympathy.

'You don't fucking mean it, you smug bastard.'

Nick nodded his head towards Matt's back. 'Shall we go into the snug?'

They picked up their pints and squeezed themselves into the tiny compartment.

'All right, old man. Tell us.'

'On her way back from Warsaw, she's stopping off in England to head for the village where he lives. She'll then presumably spend some time with him before returning. Playing at motherhood.'

Angela appeared, all six stone of her, clad in shorts and sandals, and looking peaky with the cold.

'Will you have a hot whiskey?' Jim asked. 'And you heard what I was saying. Yes, Nan has fucked off to meet her son.' Drink was making his voice audible in the other bar and Nick put his finger to his lips. 'Sure they'll all know sooner or later and I'll be the laughing stock of the parish. I can hear them. "He couldn't even give her one!"'

The Swanns exchanged looks. 'You keep saying this. And there's no need for anyone to know about it. Our lips are buttoned. We haven't even told the kids. And if they do get to know about it, so what?' Nick muttered.

Angela tucked herself on to the bus seat between them, balancing her drink on the floor. 'Here's to Nan's swift return.' She raised her glass.

Jim emitted a nasty laugh. He ordered another pint, his fourth in less than an hour.

Nick suggested they should both go to the caves the next day, 'to take your mind off things,' but Jim was too embedded in self-pity to reply. He slurped on his stout, his elbows on his knees. 'She'll fall in love with the bastard.'

'Don't be daft,' Angela said, trying to stifle a yawn.

'What would you do in her place?' Nick asked his wife.

'I think I'd refuse to see him.'

'But you haven't got a son,' Jim said.

There was an uneasy silence.

'Let's go into the other bar and discuss silage,' Nick suggested, fed up.

Nan fell asleep as soon as she got on the plane from Warsaw. The concert had been an average success, the attendance reasonable. She had mooned around the city for half a day, wanting to find a present for Jim, but either things were too shoddy or she didn't have enough *zlotys* for the more classy garments. But in truth her heart wasn't in it. She couldn't help thinking of all the times she had had such joy in buying him presents, but now . . . well, anything she brought home would probably be thrown in her face. She remembered how once, in Budapest, when he had accompanied her, she had waited at the wrong café for him and had got more and more anxious, and when finally they met up they had clung to each other like two monkeys. As she walked the streets, sticky with heat, all these memories plagued her. Do cattle know, she wondered, when they leave their fields for the last time that they'll never see them again? She tried to throw off the feeling of doom, but it was so entwined with her other feeling of anticipation that her head throbbed and her shoes hurt and she ploughed on, staring into shop windows, half seeing the contents, half contemplating a purchase. Eventually she had subsided on to a seat in the park and watched the beautiful little Polish girls and boys kick a ball around.

She woke with a jump as the plane made an uneven landing at Heathrow, and as they filtered off to collect their luggage, met by the British immigration official who checked their passports with scant courtesy, a young man with whom she'd shared a seat clicked his teeth.

God, oh, God. And God, how she hated Heathrow. It was impossible to get into or get out of, impossible to find anyone to tell her how to get to Crowsfort. She assumed the village would be scarce of public transport. She had looked at the map and ascertained that the nearest station would be Hindhead, and then a taxi? But that meant going first to London and then to where? Charing Cross? Her case got heavier and heavier until eventually she reached the tube station. Why was she doing this? She could still turn back and get an Aer Lingus flight to Dublin. She stopped in her tracks. Turned. She clattered back the way she'd come, missing signs, changing routes, running.

At the Aer Lingus desk they told her, 'Six o'clock' – a two hours wait.

'Are you sure? Please check again.'

She drifted off. Went to a tea bar and got a plastic cup of tea and a sandwich. She sat down in a row of benches beside a young woman and a baby. An unending stream of people. Some arriving, some leaving. The young woman unwrapped a bottle and put it in the baby's mouth. She sighed deeply. Irrecoverable, her past. Irreversible, her future.

It was four when she arrived at Crowsfort. A main street with a river at one end curling cleanly under a bridge. A tobacconist/newsagent, an antique shop. In the window an assortment of wrought-iron minutiae. Should she buy Jim a present here? She stopped to listen to the chimes as people moved about inside. A cake shop which was also a café. Women eating and chatting.

The Midland Bank brand new. Glass-fronted. A disguised mini-market and at last the pub. Not the Horse and Hound but the Wheatsheaf. Pseudo-Tudor with a rounded doorway and small windows with wooden frames. Apart from the name of the pub, everything was as expected. All the people she saw were either young mothers with spotless children or middle-aged ladies dressed as she should be, unhurried. A couple of pleasant-looking lads eyed her up as she walked up the steps.

Jim woke up with a severe hangover. Jesus. What had he said to the Swanns last night? He had insisted on buying a bottle of whiskey and taking it round to their house. It must have been around four when he had tottered home. The Pen had force fed him with leftovers when all he'd wanted was alcoholic oblivion. Needless to say, neither of the Swanns had been, as far as he could remember, in any way drunk. He rummaged round in his mind for any thread of memory, but he could recall nothing after opening the bottle of whiskey. Thank God neither of the Cygnets had been there to witness his debauch. He did remember singing, probably no better than Gilsenan *père*. He looked out on the day. Grey. Where was his car? Jesus, he must have left it at the pub. Luckily, he supposed. And did he walk home or did Nick drive him? Yes, he had sung in the pub.

> Love is teasing and love is easing
> And love's a pleasure when first it's new.

Sweet Jesus, who else had been there? Both the Slater brothers, he remembered, and also the eldest Gilsenan – Raphael. Poor Pat, wavering on his feet, and, dear God, Martin, Nan's inamorato. What's this he'd said to him? Something about his girlfriend having flown away like a bird in the night, and he had knocked over a full pint and Matt Rogan had swept up the broken glass, none too pleased. And who had the Swanns been talking to? Oh, Barney the Protestant. Of course, they would be. Rich like themselves and middle class for generations. Established. Not a blow-in in the place except him, ready to make a fool of himself. He reached to the top shelf, where Nan hid the painkillers. Nan. Oh, Nan. Yes, Nan was nowhere. In Kraków, of course, basking in her success, with no doubt some handsome Middle European kissing her hand, presenting her with flowers. Telling her how beautiful she was. Liars, those Poles, worse than the Irish. Taking her to a bistro or whatever they drink in, buying her liqueurs, seducing her. Jesus. He stirred three Disprins into a glass of water and waited for them to disintegrate. Should he feed the animals and go back to bed? It was already noon. He fetched the paper from the postbox but was too sick to open it. The post consisted of the usual bumph from advertisers and an invitation to an exhibition of mixed-media paintings in the town's art gallery. He listlessly read the names of the artists, most of them unfamiliar to him, and shoved it on the dresser.

PART II

A ROUND THE WOODEN BAR COUNTER there was a smattering of middle-aged men. They wore the same uniform of open-necked shirts of different colours and ill-fitting jeans. They all had 'halves' of bitter in front of them. Back from the bar there were three polished tables and chairs.

Nan ordered a gin and tonic and sat down at one of them. Nobody took any notice of her. Having ascertained that the pub was also an inn, she booked a bed for the night. She could only expect the worst. That he would arrive, look around and, spotting her, the only strange customer in the pub, dismiss her and stand up at the bar. But why should he come into the pub at all? The arrangement was that she should phone him at six. In her bag was the number. She now checked it for the hundredth time.

Her heart was doing queer things, pumping unevenly, and her clothes were sticking to her. She felt travel-dirty and she knew she must look a mess. She kept remembering Jim's words when she'd told him the news first: I won't be a surrogate father to a thirty-year-old delinquent. Or something like that. She ordered another drink.

'Mother.'

'Mother.' What does that mean? Mother of God. Mother of Pearl. Mother of Charles Henry Fordson, stranger. Again she imagined her father, that man whom she had admired, loved even, and yet he too had been a stranger. Their village also had been in awe of him. Not one of them. An outsider, a blow-in – like Jim and herself. But this Fordson, he is not a blow-in in Crowsfort. He belongs here. But did he feel odd because he had been adopted from somewhere unknown?

In all the years he had lived here, had he had an inkling that there was a quality that he possessed that was not of this place? Did his genes disturb him in some way when his parents told him that he was not their child?

One thing she knew, she must retain her dignity. Jim had spoiled her all these years. He had allowed her to be herself. But with this stranger she must put on a new coat. Plaster over the cracks. But how? God, how? The barman had now been replaced by a woman in her fifties. She assumed they were man and wife. An oldish man on the right called out, 'Another half of bitter, Doris.'

She asked Doris to point her to her room. 'Up to the top of the stairs, right. Call down if you want anything.' Nan trundled her bag into the room, glad at last to be rid of it, and sank down on the bed. A square window looked out on a back yard where barrels were stacked and crates of bottles tiered on top of each other. So unlike the back of Lawlor's with the empty iron lungs lolling among plastic bags and dog shit. She began to undress.

She had travelled in jeans and a T-shirt but now, after a shower, she'd have to consider what to wear. What would he want her to be? Swinging Sixties? One of the cake-eating women? She searched the mirror for grey hairs and ran her fingers through them.

She bundled the rest of her hair on top of her head and got into the shower. Feeling refreshed, she stood a while by the window, naked. She yanked it open to get some air. The weather in England hadn't broken like at home. It was humid in the little room.

She threw everything out of her bag and tried on one of the dresses she'd brought. Boring, beige, mid-length cotton. In the mirror she saw a different woman. A woman in her forties, handsome, all right, but much older than the woman in T-shirt and jeans. She tore the dress off, putting on a plain white blouse. Why hadn't she brought a skirt? Should she search the village for one? She pulled out a pair of white cotton trousers and put them on. She looked ridiculous. All in white. Like a nurse or a butcher's assistant. She tore them off and put back on her jeans. She turned this way and that, tried to straighten her hands, which were rolled into fists. The good the shower had done her had ebbed away. She must phone him. Now. Yes, now!

Fumbling with the English coins, she put some extra ten-penny pieces in, afraid of being cut off if he answered. If he answered. She listened to the *brr-brr* of the ringing tone, little rivers of sweat running down between her breasts, into her ribcage. He's out. He's changed his mind. She pictured him watching the phone, unable to pick it up. Then it clicked.

'Hello.'

'Hello.'

'This is Nan. Nan McDonald.'

A moment's silence and then a near-inaudible 'Yes?'

'I've arrived.' The instrument was wet and she wiped it on her blouse. 'I ... er ... Where can we meet? I'm in the Wheat-sheaf. Booked in. That *is* Charles?'

'Yes.'

'Then can we meet here?'

Silence.

'Very well. I'll be down.'

The line went dead.

She stood in the little alcove at the back of the bar. As from another world she heard the normal pub noises, the clatter of glasses, the laughter. She must have another drink, must jack up her courage somehow or other. Charles. I am your . . . Your what?

'A pint of best bitter, please.'

'Here you are.'

She carried the drink over to the table. Some of the customers looked casually at her and then returned to their drinks.

'I don't want to meet this man.' The sentence drummed at her. 'I do not want to . . . I can't cope. Dear God.' She turned and twisted in her chair, searching the door as people filtered in. She hadn't smoked for months but she longed for a cigarette. She kept tidying things, settling her handbag more neatly by her feet, picking up her drink and replacing the beer mat in an exact position.

Two women had come in and they sat down at the adjacent table. One of the women should have been her. Tall, angular, sharp nose, healthy-eyed. Strong mid-forties, in a blue blouse and flared skirt, interesting hair, combed slightly to one side.

But her companion was different. Broad face, a little humped, with straight brown hair which she swept off her face every few minutes . . . What did they have in common? Sex? Maybe. She liked the look of them. The older woman had a wide mouth, with the slightest lift of amusement in the corners. Nan needed a friend. A friend! She had no friends.

Somewhere in her other life . . . One day . . . If ever . . . Up till now, Jim had been her friend. She had never found the need for a circle of women friends, never one for morning meetings in coffee shops. The daft locals had been enough for her because behind it all was Jim. But . . .

A young man came through the door.

She rose. She watched him order a drink at the bar. He looked round, noticed her and went back to the counter. She sat back down.

The older woman looked over at her, gave her a sympathetic nod. Nan felt a terrible pain behind her eyes. She clutched the side of the table.

She found herself at the bar again, ordering another pint.

There were two layers of people standing now, couples flirting. One of the women had a squawky laugh, which went up the scale like a cockerel crowing. Good chaps and gals telling jokes. Stale old jokes. Nan shakily wove her way back to the table.

Maybe he wouldn't come. But suddenly she was looking at him. He was there, her son. There. Surveying the people around him. Not drinking. He spoke to Doris and she nodded in Nan's direction. He walked over. She half rose, clutching the table with her left hand. He looked down at her without speaking.

God, she was looking at his blood father. The strictly Roman cut of the Caesars in her Latin book. He wasn't dark, as she had expected him to be. Had been once. His hair had a wilful little twist at the back of his neck. Light brown, nearly chestnut. And there was something else she noticed immediately. He was not pleased with what he saw. Did not take her proffered hand.

She was standing. Fully. Facing him.

'So, we meet at last.' She broke the silence. 'Do you like to stay, have a drink, or go somewhere else?'

He shrugged.

They went out and took a turn off the main street. She must have suggested they eat something. They walked stiffly, occasionally knocking against each other on the narrow footpath. When they did, they apologised. Or was it just she who said sorry, once or twice?

A teenager on her first date, mortified by her wrong clothes, her wrong hair, her wrong face. Taking two short steps to match his long ones, or uncomfortable strides, ungainly, unfeminine.

And then down another turn, a small butt of a road that ended in a picturesque yard with an orange-lit sign saying Harry's Bistro.

Jim started to attack his neglected garden. He dug over the lettuce bed where the army of slugs had feasted. Propped up his peas and tied a trellis round the runner beans. For the last four nights he'd been drunk at closing time. He had discussed Formula One motor racing with much lack of erudition. There were whisperings about a pending legal battle between McCarthy and the Slaters. At one point Fonsie had said to Jim, 'With your money you should get a speed boat. I'd say your missus would be good at the water-skiing.' Jim had been too lethargic to answer the barb. He'd heard it all before. Rich blow-ins, even though they'd been here nearly ten years.

Damn it, he missed Nan. What had got into him to be so nasty to her? A son is no big deal. After all, if he'd known about the child in the beginning it wouldn't have made a ha'p'orth of difference. Is it just that there's no room for change? Is that it? Is their relationship not solid enough to ride the upheaval?

Supposing it were the other way around? Supposing some middle-aged woman turned up with a grown-up daughter whom he had sired as many years ago? What would Nan's reaction be? What would he expect her to do? Act like he'd been acting over the last weeks? Spitefully childish. Mind you, a beautiful young daughter appearing out of the blue might really throw a spanner in the works! He sniggered to himself as he plunged his arm into a clump of nettles.

Was it the drink? Carrying on like this just piled up his panic, making him a target for the likes of Fonsie Slater's barbs. He should have told him to fuck off and mind his own business. He had been conscious of staggering on the way to the jacks, trying to seem sober.

Five pints of stout and then the shorts. How many? And now the shagging car was still at the pub. Actually it was Fonsie who had driven him home. Ambiguities!

'Tonight,' he addressed the spade, 'I'll just fetch the car, come straight home and go to bed early.'

The telephone rang.

They went through the wrought-iron gateway into the little courtyard. There were trestle tables and chairs dotted among trailing plants. Nan suggested they go inside. She felt vulnerable in the twilit air, needed plainness and electricity.

They were led into the interior by a possibly Greek waiter, who took them to a table with a flourish. They appeared to be the only customers and Nan was sat into her chair with a bump.

Charles picked up the menu and, as though he were reading from it, said, 'The organisation said you were a pianist.'

'I am ... I've just got back from Kraków.' She studied her own menu. 'I'm very excited to meet you.'

The expression on his face didn't change.

'I mean, did you have a job tracing ... I mean, what prompted ...' Words were doubling back on themselves. She sat on the edge of her silly seat. The motifs in the restaurant were wrought iron and greenery, and the back of her chair, with its plaited metal hoops, knocked against her spine.

Little snippets of conversation were gobbled up by gaps of silence. A bottle of retsina, should have, but didn't, loosen their tongues.

To her query as to whether he was married or had a partner, he replied that he had lived with a married woman for a while, but her children had been so obnoxious they'd made it hell for him, remarking, 'Children always win, don't they?'

There were caustic statements, such as his father was the workhorse, pulled the cart all his life. And no, his mother didn't have a career.

Going back through the village he mentioned that he had been in the car when his parents were killed and Nan was stunned into monosyllabic horror. How? God! Her mind filled with the pictures of molten metal, bodies being cut out, ambulances screaming, as again she tried to meet his strides on the narrow footpath.

She followed him to his house, passing the Wheatsheaf and taking a sweep of the town through a small park and out into a clump of semi-detached houses ringed round cultivated flowerbeds. His house was at the far side and she was surprised to see how unkempt it was compared with the rest of them. Could this really be the family house?

Miss Charity's words rang in her head. 'Hupper class, from what I 'ear. Give him a chance . . .' Like in a lottery.

She followed him into the drab sitting room, where a 40-watt bulb in a china shade hung from the ceiling and barely lit up the myriad pieces of furniture, the three-piece suite, upholstered in striped whipcord, and the unlit standard lamp in the corner, with its shade like an old woman's petticoat. Yet Charles, home now, took up a stance by the empty grate, his elbow on the mantelpiece, like a soldier posing for a photograph.

'I have nothing to offer you. I eat out since my parents died.'

'It's all right.'

He asked her if she wanted to give them a tune.

Of course, the second thing Nan had noticed was the up-right in the corner. She got up, laughing, and leafed through the dusty sheets of music scattered on the lid. All the old favourites: Beethoven's *Für Elise* and Moonlight Sonata, Brahms's Lullaby, Chopin's waltzes.

She turned round to look at him. 'I don't think so,' she said.

Jim rushed in to answer the phone before it got the call-answering service. He grabbed the receiver. 'Yes?'

'If you want your dog you can come and get him.'

Slater. Shotgun Slater. Jesus, Jesus. He slammed the phone down and rushed out again. Fuck, no car. He stumbled across the field, smelling slurry mixed with cut grass. Jesus. No. Please, God, no. His breath rasped as he tripped in the hoof marks round the gate.

Fonsie at the door with a smirk on his face. 'I threw it in the sheuch.'

'You threw Shep? You threw Shep into the sheuch?'

Fonsie lit a cigarette.

The sheuch! The fucking ditch! Jim skirted the field and went out on the road. He drifted along. The door of Rogan's was shut. Matt was gone for his tea. He would drive home in the car. Drive to hell. Drive to Lawlor's. Without the keys. No keys. He leant against the immobile machine.

Eventually Matt breezed up in his Escort. The back number plate, askew, bounced as he did a U-turn.

As he unbarred the front door, Jim said, 'My dog got shot.'

Matt had been a small farmer before he became a publican. He believed dogs should be locked in. He himself had an Alsatian, a miserable yoke who never saw further than the railings of his pen. He clattered around in the Stygian darkness, turning on the telly full volume.

Jim wondered about suicide but said instead, 'Have you ever thought of Australia?' Matt had a son there.

Matt smiled, through his crooked yellow teeth, looking like a broken-down member of the Mafia.

'One? Pint?'

'And a half-one.'

'Neil Donaghy was found dead in his house,' Matt mentioned as he pulled the pint.

'But he was young.' Jim was confused. 'How?'

'Dunno. He was found sitting in his chair. He was supposed to go to the mart with Jack Swift, who went down to fetch him. He had to break in through the window.'

Jim felt meek in the face of this news. He had liked Neil very much. A quiet man of courtly manner. A man who you couldn't imagine bad-mouthing anyone. 'Shit,' Jim said. 'Shit.' He drank the whiskey neat and started on his pint.

'I left my keys in the house.' Marooned in this dark hole, all he wanted to do was to go home and sit by the telephone.

Where were the photographs? Where was his past? She felt a madness of love and pity for this person she didn't know. Might never know. There was nothing on the wall except a picture of a shipwreck in a gilt frame. Had he burnt all the memorabilia when his parents died? As she leafed through the music, he stood there with an urbane expression, as though what he thought of as a career woman was beneath contempt.

She suddenly said, 'I'm Nanny Wine and you were born on 20 May 1962. In a charity home for fallen women in Cheapside, London. I had a friend called Elsie. And there was a broken piano on which I played, "In the Mood" and "Hound Dog".'

Jim went into the back bar to get cigarettes. Fonsie Slater came in simultaneously. Jim felt his head getting light, as if he were about to topple over. 'You fucking cunt,' he screamed. 'You fucking bastard.' In the dimness of his mind, Jim knew now that things were not working out, but he couldn't stop himself from going at Fonsie, head on. 'Why did you do it?' he screamed, nearly falling in his own onslaught.

Matt came out of the side of the bar and Jim was pushed back against the machine.

'You poor craythur,' Fonsie sneered.

Jim ran into the toilet. He had to hold on to the wall to steady himself.

A while later, because logic could only be restored by the

intake of more alcohol, he crept out. Pretending normality, he sat back at the bar, ordered a pint.

'I'm sorry,' he said to Matt. 'It's just that I worry about Nan when she hears about the dog. I was out of order.'

Matt, engrossed in the telly, was half listening. 'The missus away?' he asked for the second time.

'Aye. Poland.'

'It's well for some.'

Why do people, when they hear about someone travelling, always say this? He, Jim, loved his home. Like all blow-ins, he loved passionately his new life.

Thinking of his house and his animals, it seemed as though his days, so perfect in their repetition, had been wiped away like a theorem on a blackboard.

Before he knew what had happened it was closing time. How could it be? In an amorphous blur he had drifted from one bar to another. Flotsam.

Charles was unfazed by her outburst, merely said, 'I don't doubt you.'

'I just wondered. Did you think I was an impostor?'

'Who gave you that notion?' He laughed.

Nan felt she could go no further. Fatigued by the travelling and the emotional stress, all she wanted then was to lie down, to hide her head away from the prying eyes. She bade him good night, suggesting a coffee in the morning.

Wandering through the empty street, she said to herself, 'Tomorrow I'll go home and we will have met for the first time in thirty years. The future perfect. The perfect future.'

But once in her room in the pub she only looked at the telephone. Where would Jim be now? In Rogan's, at the Swanns', in bed? Did she really have another life somewhere or had she murdered the past? Murdered herself for a stranger. She'd just passed through a non-event. A drastically important non-event. She couldn't find the thin line of blood that tied herself to this man. There in that hotel bar, thirty-one years ago, she'd run the back of her bare arm down the back of that stranger's father's arm, the strap of her bra falling over her shoulder. And he also had been a stranger. How she had asked for it, her body limp with excitement as she followed him into his room, a drunken fifteen-year-old. The skin of their two bodies. Her first orgasm. Just like the Caesars in her Latin book.

Yes, that had been the first time.

And she had sworn it would never happen again.

Until.

My God, Jim, she thought. And the thought slammed her back into the present.

That seed sown was walking about after the big gap of years in this delightfully normal English village.

How bridge the gap? How not?

She dialled Ireland.

'Neither Nan nor Jim can come to the phone at the moment. Please leave a message after the bleep. Thank you.'

She replaced the receiver.

Jim woke up, the sunshine pouring through his uncurtained window. Bile came into his mouth when he tried to rise. He fell back into the bed, swallowing and retching. The horror of the previous night came at him. What had he done? Said? Had he sung 'Oh love is teasing and love is easing . . .'? Oh, Jesus!

Again!

Had he sung that? With his arm around Fonsie? No. No. And flirted with Greta.

Oh, no!

Standing in the toilet in this abject state, he watched the yellow pee trickle into the pan. Here he was, fully dressed in the same clothes he'd worn for the last four days. If only Fonsie could see him now! He could kill himself for being such a toady.

Should he drive to the quarry and throw himself into that murderous black hole? It had often struck him that he could do this if Nan were to die before him. They had planned if either of them had a terminal disease they would make a suicide pact. But Nan wasn't dead. He fumbled with the lavatory chain and the cistern howled like a liner leaving the docks.

He went down to the kitchen.

Jesus.

Once again his car was at the pub.

Who had driven him home? The evening must have culminated in his telling everyone he was sober enough to drive.

McCarthy.

McCarthy was there. Did McCarthy leave him home in his tractor. Or was it Matt Rogan himself? Surely he'd remember if he'd come home in a tractor! He put on the electric kettle.

Fonsie! What had he said to him? That he understood why he'd shot Shep. That it was only Nan he had been thinking of. Worrying about her there in unfriendly Poland, earning their crust. He didn't want her to come home to a dead dog. In the sheuch. The cunt, the fucking cunt. And he, miserable chicken-livered Jim, had told the bastard, he understood. Almost said he was right to shoot the pest. Dogs were a curse.

A hen jumped on the windowsill. Fucking birds. Always hungry. And not a blade of grass for the heifers in this drought. He made the sink in a quick dive and put the last three painkillers in his mouth while swallowing a glass of water. Yes, it was McCarthy. And not in his tractor. That awful-looking dark green Fiat he drove, with the broken passenger seat. Francis McCarthy, always wanting to dispose of something. Sheep. And now he still had no car. And no Swanns to save him. At least they'd have known the reason for his debauch, his misery. He turned on the radio. The fruity voice of Gay Byrne's sidekick was discussing with a nun the ongoing revelations of past cruelties to unmarried mothers and their offspring having been 'sold' to American couples. He switched it off. That was all he needed to press the needle more firmly into his nerve ends. Jesus. Why doesn't she ring? He checked the answering machine again and was told he had no new messages. And Shep. Oh, God. Shep. What was he going to do?

The hen was back on the windowsill. He'd feed the fowl. And the heifers. That's right. Then walk to the pub when there was no possibility of its being open. He'd flagellate himself with sobriety. Today cold turkey. No Swanns, no Matt Rogan. And dear Jesus, Neil. He'd have to go to the removal. Just go to the church and be seen and straight home.

The heatwave was back. The two days of rain had brought smiles to the countryside. Forty shades of green and beautiful with it. As a child he'd been a real sissy, loving to collect thimbles of dew on a summer's morning to feed the fairies. Jesus. Were his senses deserting him? Thinking about fairies and thimbles full of dew. He tottered to the sheds and scooped out the hen food as the fowl raced across the yard. And slopping water in the bucket, he dragged it, spilling into his shoes, to the heifers.

Nan woke early and jumped into the shower. Alternatively roasting and freezing herself and soaking the bathroom floor, she demisted the mirror and inspected her glassy body. This morning she must dress like a middle-aged mother. This morning she felt different. Angry. She would surprise him with her ambiguities, her talent for change. She decided to put on one of the other dresses she'd brought. The striped silk one, a madly expensive purchase she'd once made in Barcelona, and it was not too short – just above the knee. She carefully made up her eyes, her only sacrifice to cosmetic disguise, and went down to breakfast.

Passing through the bar, with its smells of ashtrays and spilt liquor, she went into the dining room. There were two other residents and they sat in the corner at the cereal and fruit stage. The man's face was red as a raspberry and the woman grey and fidgety. She imagined her lying at the edge of the bed, terrified of his raspberry claws creeping towards her.

Neither spoke. Perhaps they hadn't spoken for years. With anguish, she thought of herself and Jim and how their early-morning chat, which had always been the nicest part of their day, had become stilted and bitchy. Would they end up like this couple? She scooped grapefruit segments into a bowl. The waitress came – not Doris – and she ordered toast and tea, afraid of the breakfast and her experiences in Irish hotels and in Heathrow, waiting between planes.

When the couple passed she said good morning. They didn't answer.

Charles smiled at the waitress. He was easy here. Familiar with a place where things were provided without pain.

'The usual,' he said.

She ordered coffee and joined him.

The café was pleasant and airy. A light breeze blew the curtain into the room. She wanted to secure herself somehow in this odyssey but no words seemed to fit. Eventually she told him that she had to leave at eleven and that, if he liked, she might visit him again in the near future.

'I pass through England frequently.'

'What's it like in Ireland?' His breakfast had arrived – a full fry – and he was buttering a piece of toast.

'Ireland? Oh, where I live. I told you – it's pleasant enough. A small community. Eccentrics. Oddities . . .' Her voice trailed. What had happened to this man down the years? What had dammed him up? His eyes, hard as opals, caused ripples of anxiety up her spine. 'You hate me,' she blurted, feeling wizened with unshed tears. 'And you think this was a mistake.'

'On the contrary. And I hate nobody.'

She rose, shoving her paper napkin under her saucer. 'You have my address.'

In the street her eyes were scalded by the light. The town was waking up. Women who had left their children to school were talking in groups. Vans were delivering goods. Trays of bread and cakes were being carried into the supermarket. A man put a sign for newspapers outside his shop. She hurried on to the Wheatsheaf to collect her bag.

At Hindhead the platform was deserted, the commuters long gone. 'Which platform?' she asked as she bought her ticket, but she got no reply. She looked at the screen. The London train was due in twenty minutes.

So they had come for him with all that baby gear. Frilled bonnets, blue-ribboned jackets – soft wool and fluffy cotton. And she hadn't been allowed to see them – that was the rule. But she had imagined them, tall and clean. A childless couple in their thirties. And she'd handed him over in his charity clothes without putting on the new ones she'd been given. A lump had caught in her throat. But she hadn't cried. His lungs were busting with angry sobs. Elsie, also, shed tears. Elsie had cried for him, Nanny Wine's child. She had felt heady when Elsie had held her and she had remained dry-eyed. The lost year that had dragged her into the depths – an unending inferno – was clipped off like a piece of paper and forgotten. So she had gone to the piano to play to Elsie. To cheer Elsie up. With Jelly Roll Morton's 'Grandpa Spells', the notes like coins falling into a tin bucket, and she'd told Elsie that when she got a job she'd come to see her. 'You'll never!' 'I will, I promise.' And Elsie had cried more, because her parents had been killed in the war when she was tiny. Obliterated by a bomb when she'd been sent to a farm for safety. And how she had searched. Never believing in their death. And in her loneliness after the war, had gone from job to job, man to man, and eventually got knocked up. She wanted to straighten herself out and keep the child, she'd told her. That's why she'd had such sympathy for Nan's dilemma. 'And you'll be back,' Miss Charity had said. 'They all come back.' 'No, Miss, never.' 'Another bun in the oven, like as not.' 'No, Miss, never.'

Beyond the platform the tracks danced in the sunlight as her train snaked slowly in.

Well, he made it. Made it to the pub without dying or vomiting on the way. The heat exacerbated his hangover. He leant over his car thankfully, having opened the driver's door to let in some air, afraid to suffocate in this greenhouse of a machine. And who should pass only Francie McCarthy in his tractor.

'You were well scuttered,' Francie shouted, his tractor throwing dust into his face.

The doors of Rogan's were firmly shut and Jim thought if he were religious he would cross himself, but instead he turned on the ignition and, watery-eyed, drove home.

It was Nan on the phone. He'd heard it ringing and he'd tripped on the mat as he rushed in.

'Jim?'

'Indeed.' About time.

'I've been ringing you for ages.'

'I was fetching the car.'

'Why, what happened? Did it break down?'

'No, I did.'

'Drunk in Rogan's?'

'A clever guess, don't you think?'

'I'm on my way. Will you meet me at Knock at five? I'm

running out of coins.'

Elated, he put the phone down. He stood at the window. A wood pigeon swooped on to the wire netting of the hen run and called *coooo, coooo*. Early in their love career, they'd fucked each other in an empty room in Harcourt Terrace and a pigeon had called his call and Jim said to Nan, 'He's telling you something. I love you. I love you.' He watched the pigeon now, scratching under his wing with his beak, plumping out his feathers, obscenely sexy. He would fuck Nan tonight like a buck rabbit. Like a buck rabbit he'd fuck. And his mind zigzagged into all the different places they had fucked. That awful flat in Adelaide Road with the brown linoleum and broken sink. But no. That wasn't the worst place. Upper Mount Street. Jesus ... And the old lady, Auntie Vi, they'd called her, who always said, 'Turn off the light.' (They'd shared the kitchen, and he made her toast every morning.) And Merrion Street, where the recent occupant's dog had left his turds and eaten half the floor and the fleas had danced in the sunbeams like hayseed. And how everything was funny as they sucked and munched each other. And then there was Mrs Noone with the one eye, who lent them her luxurious pad for half a week so that they would mind her bird. And what a fucking noise the bird made. Nan threatened to get the taxidermist who lived in that lane off Leeson Street to it. And they'd laughed some more.

Surely they were blessed?

But Shep's in the sheuch. Dead. Dear God. Nan wont let me fuck her because I let Shep die. He'd have to have a pint. Just one. The one pint before going to Knock. It was an hour and a half to Knock. Petrol, shower, clean clothes. His head jumped and he hiccuped as he stood in the bathroom, peeling off his stinking underwear and socks. 'Nan is not a mother.' He spoke out loud. Twice. 'Nan is not a mother.' The water hit him, red-hot needles. Mad hot. He laid back his head and let it pour over his neck and chest, soaping his hair, his eyes stinging as he blindly reached for a cloth. Out of the shower, his head was better. Not cured, but better. The pigeon said *coooo, coooo* and puffed out his chest. Pouted. A pouter pigeon. He threw his dirty clothes into the wash basket, and in the bedroom, opened the windows and pulled the sheets off the bed. He had to sit then. Stay very quiet for a minute. To get his balance. My balance, he said. I'm fine. He took a handful of the mattress and raised himself up. He thought of Pat Mullen, who never sat down. Once he had asked him why and he'd said it was because of the piles. 'It's nice to be nice,' he said. 'It's nice to be a bollocks.' He addressed the walls: 'I'd appreciate it if you'd stay still.' He waited. In the car he'd be all right. He'd be all right in the car.

He'd get to the basilica of his mind and say a prayer to Mary Queen of Heaven. Please keep the walls of Babylon from falling on me and make Nan's plane glide safely on to the runway. He was clean now, combed and shaved. Clean as a candle. And frightened with it.

On the tube to Heathrow, Nan remembered. She remembered when she'd gone back to the hostel to see Elsie and found her gone. 'Where is she?' she'd screamed at Miss Charity. 'Where is Elsie?' 'You back? Didn't take you long to get knocked up.' 'Miss, where? Tell me. Her address.' 'Think I keep labels on you when you leave?' 'Surely, Miss, she left a message for me? She was my friend.' 'Not what she said when you'd gone.'

She walked through the mayhem that is Heathrow, the tannoy shouting incomprehensibles, remembering Charity's words: 'Not what she said when you'd gone.' But she lied. She must have lied. The absurdity of time perplexed her as she stood at the baggage check-in. That was yesterday those words said. Those lies lied. Not thirty years ago and the dark-haired infant stiff with fury being handed over. His name erased from history. Séan Wine into Charles Henry Fordson. And now that latent anger. That crushed anger, hidden all those years, surfaced at their meeting. Yesterday? Yes, yesterday.

The tannoy roared, the noughts on the clock turned into four nought one. Passengers stood in exasperated layers bound for all parts of the globe – Kazakhstan, Bombay, Brussels, Istanbul, Paris, Madrid, Knock. Digital clocks with their ever-changing numbers saying, 'Not what she said when you'd gone.'

And Charles Henry Fordson, stranger, son of Nanny Wine, sauntering back into the past, up the street, in the village of Crowsfort in the county of Surrey, England.

PART III

A S WEEKS PASSED AFTER HER RETURN Nan tried to settle.
Since Jim refused to listen to what he called her adventures, she had to dam up the memory of those wasted days. In public they skated on the surface of normality, but at home wearisome silences punctuated their exchanges.

The long hot summer had tailed off into autumn. As the leaves turned and snapped off, squalls of rain came down from the hills. Although they helped each other mend fences, tie back blackthorn, when they'd finished they'd return to their individual rooms and shut themselves in.

Sometimes Jim stood outside Nan's door, listening to her practising, repeating a passage over and over again, the music opening out like the very voice of melancholy. But then he'd creep away, demoralised, having no idea why he did this.

In similar manner, Nan might hover outside his study, words staccato in her head, afraid to turn the handle.

One day their faces played with brief smiles when Nan suggested they might get a puppy. 'Shep was a good dog,' Jim muttered. But the notion became too intimate for them to bear.

Even so, cracks were appearing. They both sensed that they were on the verge of something which as yet they daren't put a name to.

As they drove to the pub of a blustery evening they'd catch each other laughing if, say, Onion-head wiggled past on his bike – 'The cut of him. Like a plucked seagull' – or Ralph Gilsenan, his eyes hiding years of hopeless inheritance – 'There he goes, the bollocks, claiming another rood off McCarthy's.'

Yes, they really believed the wound of the year past was on its way to healing.

One day Nan ventured, 'So I met him. And it wasn't a success.'

Jim shrugged. 'So?'

'So nothing.' No more was said.

She played in Waterford in October, but by the time November came winter was howling round them, a beast ready to devour all before it.

Matt Rogan said he'd never seen the like and they shivered over their drinks. The old people began to die. 'When the leaf snaps and when the bud quickens' was the saying around here. Hugh McGorman, Nan's friend, was the first, Old Gilsenan the next. Raphael divided the house into two and sibling hatred ran unstinted between them. Jim and Nan attended the funerals, the wakes, stood by the graves, blowing on their fingers, repairing to Rogan's to drink hot whiskeys in the fading light.

As they worked up to Christmas they talked of 'doing something different this year'. Jim had a pile of brochures on the table that he'd written for. 'What about Tunisia?' He ruffled through them. 'Cheap for a week and full board.' But Nan looked at him, trying to stop her cup from shaking. Then he saw it. Saw the English postmark. And he knew.

'You've betrayed me,' he shouted. 'Again. After I thought … I thought … You were so … all right … calm … I thought –'

'I never promised anything. You never asked me. You wouldn't talk to me.'

'But you said –'

'I said nothing . . . That's the whole point.'

Jim picked up the brochures and threw them into the waste-paper basket, kicking it with a, 'Fuck you. Fuck you anyway.'

She ran from the room and locked herself in her study.

She put the letter on top of the piano and began to play. After twenty minutes she slammed down the lid and burst into tears. Her sobs came in uncontrolled gulps which shook and twisted her body. She would cry all day like this, sitting at the silent piano. She would weep till her body was shredded and limp, till a cancer grew inside her and clawed its way into her heart.

In the kitchen Jim sat white like a corpse, the newspaper unread in his lap, the coffee cooling on the table.

He heard her sobs but could not move to go to her. Why was she crying, anyway? Wasn't this what she wanted – to insinuate her son's presence into his life? He banged the paper against his chair. Maybe it's news of his death, he thought, and with the thought a little shiver ran through him. Yes, that was it. If he wanted to see her, would he not have written long ago? And that was why Nan wept. Wept for the death of her son who was never a son and could now never be.

The storm was battering the windowpanes. He leant over to poke the stove, to encourage a little more heat into the room. Jesus, the cold – 10 December and three more months of this. This darkness, the daylight pale in its few short hours. He listened to the *thrum, thrum* of a branch as it slid on the tin roof of the henhouse, the creaking sighs of the spruce, the rattle of an upstairs window. He knew he should get up and feed the animals, but he sat on. And on. It was already dark and she had eaten nothing all day. On an impulse he picked up the phone.

'As a medical adviser, I suppose. Not a drinking friend in Rogan's pub.'

She was conscious of her swollen face as Jim put on the central light. The doctor's arrival had given him the impetus to follow him in. 'I'm not a pretty sight, Nick, but I don't need anything, thanks.'

'Yes. I understand.'

'Do you? I've been sobbing all day. And you say you understand. Well, what do you understand?'

'You are angry with Jim.'

'If we talk at all I think it's best we talk alone. This is not a marriage guidance interview. I shall try not to be belligerent. I just don't know what to do, and words don't help.'

Nick looked over at Jim, meeting his eyes, which the latter lowered. Jim now knew what was in the letter. Not news of his death, as he had hoped, but that he wanted to come here. To this, his haven, to interfere with his life, his passionate love for the place, to destroy the vestiges of his and Nan's relationship, a glimpse of which had begun to return. No doubt Swann would say he was overreacting, but Swann's language was not his, and, as Nan just said, words don't help. All this time he had been standing in the doorway, trying to breathe evenly, thinking if he just gave one word things could continue normally. The heifers would grow, the chickens would lay, he would make good coffee in the mornings while they teased each other and planned their day. But words stuck in his gullet. He dreaded a confrontation with her which might only end in a shouting match.

Nan had cried herself out. It was as if the part of her that had walked the street with her load those years ago, and that had never cried, that had worked and paid for her music lessons, that had finally handed over her burden and walked free without a backward glance, had spilled out the lonely torture of those months. She wanted to cry out to her husband and the doctor, 'You don't understand. How can you possibly understand? But instead she leant on sarcasm as a shield for the very real pain that possessed her.

The two men stood looking at her as though they expected a transformation brought on by their superior presence. Finally she spoke the words they both dreaded. 'He wants to come here.' The men continued to stare. They watched her pick up the letter, which had lain all this time on the piano. 'He says – ' she felt a little bolder now – 'that his life is beset with minor miseries. Affidavits and wills to be sorted, and the house is rotting away – I saw that – and a visit to Ireland might be the solution. It is strange. This letter is more normal than his conversation when we met. Then he was full of innuendo and sarcasm. In fact, as I tried to tell you Jim, and you wouldn't listen. He didn't even say goodbye. So I just walked rudely out the coffee shop.'

'I will feed the animals.' Jim left the room.

Nan looked into the doctor's face. With her eyes, she beseeched him to tell her what she should do. But Swann turned his head away. To him they were fast turning into a fractious and spoilt couple who up till now had had everything handed to them on a plate. He wanted to tell her that Jim's heavy drinking was no help. It only exacerbated his lack of understanding. But he left it.

Nan got up and prowled back and forth, stopping from time to time to look at him. 'Should I talk to Angela?' she muttered as she paced.

'No. Angela would be sympathetic but she can't be you. As far as I can see, you have to let him come.'

She grew silent again, remembering the prizes she had won in the various fleadhs, remembering her first concert in a church hall in Phibsboro and how all the nervous apprehension which she had felt then was as nothing to how she felt today.

Swann started up again. 'It's only another man, after all, coming to stay. If you look on it that way. Treat him like a visitor.'

She told him there was nothing left to say and not to waste any more of his time. 'Thank you for coming.'

The doctor collected his wits. It had been an exhausting afternoon. As he left the house there was no sign of Jim. No car either. He knew what that meant.

On her own at last, Nan re-read the letter. It was as she had said, full of normality. If his real self is in this letter, she thought, his staying here might pose little problem. But what if he showed only that schizophrenic side of him, that dismissive manner, which she could not imagine Jim putting up with? What then? Supposing he refused to leave? She started pacing again. At least her tears had dried up. What was all that about? That racked body had come from somewhere very deep and distant. How she had pondered whether she should rear the baby herself. Give up her career, her love of freedom, make the normal maternal sacrifice. It would have meant never seeing her father again, or her sister or brothers. But why lie now? She had not wanted any child, she, the runt of the family, the wild girl who got into all sorts of scrapes, whom the local boys despised, thought an easy lay, although she had gone with none of them. She had always given the public a chosen persona, when underneath she had really envied her sister's ease of manner, her ability to make small exciting talk when she was tongue-tied. And finally she had loosened herself from that terrible year, a year that was lost in her calendar, that not one person in Ireland had known about, and returned to pick up where she'd left off. And found Jim. As her thoughts ended in this circle she remembered how they had loved. How they had scratched and mauled each other, and how jealous she used to be if he so much as looked at another woman, and now there he was, fucked off to the pub, without an inch of sympathy in his body or mind, without a need for her any more, only his own egotistical self. How could poor Swann possibly sort them out?

She wandered into the kitchen. So neat and alien, like

another country. The crocks were stacked away, the draining board scrubbed, the chairs tucked under the table, the floor swept. She shuffled about, looked at the unplugged kettle, the pretty tea caddie she'd bought on her travels – Spain, wasn't it? She pulled out a chair and stood with her hand on its back, her eyes unfocused. She imagined her son arriving in a taxi. Slowly getting out with his baggage. She imagined him standing outside as she went to open the door and how, once in, he would take off his coat and lay it carefully on a chair. And she would break the silence with clumsy gestures, and chance remarks about the weather, his journey, and how her husband, Jim, would welcome him later.

But Jim wouldn't be here, would he? So she'd welcome him alone, her long-lost son. Shit. What did all that mean? He was not her son. He was the son of that decent couple, that decent God-fearing couple who had reared him, guiltily making up for the lack of bloodline but without the hatred or love that is what all families share till death intervenes.

But . . .

He had once been hers . . . She had held that dark creature, that dark pulsating animal, in her arms. She had convinced herself that she had never wanted to see him again once he had gone through that door into that no man's land . . . But . . .

But she *had* met him again. And found what?

An only child who never made friends with his peers. Who botched his only relationship. What was it he'd said? Children always win? Why had they not adopted a sister for him? Of course, I've no family, wasn't I found under a stone? He'd said that also.

She walked up and down the kitchen. She filled the kettle. She stared at it. She poured some whiskey into a glass. She stared at it.

The wind had dropped. The house had settled into silence.

It was pitch black outside. The blackness of night that

hurries after the blackness of morning. The birth of light in between. The shock of birth.

Jim had ordered a pint and a half-one before he'd heard the news. Or rather the intelligence had communicated itself to his brain.

'Where?'

'In the ditch, about half eight this morning.'

'Within three feet of where Séan was found two years ago.'

'And Raphael, how's he coping?' Jim heard himself say. Somehow Jim knew. That Raphael had killed the last rival to the farm and it would never be proven. Or had he?

'Marty left around twelve with a bottle of whiskey. Seemingly he went round to Pat's and they sat drinking till around four o'clock. Pat thinks that's when he left, but how would he know the time? They were both out of it when they left here.'

'Was Raphael here when they left?' Jim asked.

There was silence while all stared at the telly. Jim's mind tried to grapple with this extraordinary happening. He ordered his second pint, when only halfway down the first. Murder in the parish. That'll make everyone sit up. A talking point over the next six months. Or, on the other hand, a point of silence. The invisible thread of suspicion. But supposing it was an accident. Supposing it wasn't Raphael but the selfsame Marty who had killed Séan, and the death had tortured him till finally he decides to commit suicide with the intention of choosing the same ditch to die in? The same ditch into which he'd thrown his brother two years ago?

As a sleuth Jim thought he might outsmart the others. But ... It was a nasty business. The Gilsenans were unpopular. No luck about that house, it was said. Raphael and his four-wheel drive. Raphael and his long face and permanent frown. He could knock back the pints, too. The last out, the final pint well paid for in advance, which he could retrieve personally from behind the counter long after Rogan had stopped serving. And slouch off into the night, his shoulders a little hunched, his chin thrust forward. The look of an owl with a broken wing. But . . . Could they all be wrong? Was it Marty, in comparison the debonair one, who carried the guilty load, and Raphael, the eldest, the most responsible, who knew? And now Marty was dead and his secret with him.

Jim was lucky his land had not been involved in a feud in the past. It had lain fallow for nearly five years. The previous owner, who was a bachelor without living relatives, had passed away and the bank had seized it and sold it to him, cheap at the price. Just before the German boom had begun. Or rather sold it to Nan. But Jim's thoughts glossed over this quickly. What's hers is mine, what's mine is hers. He sat up and ordered a third pint. He was soothed by the alcohol and this exciting news.

Forgetting the gut-wrenching chaos he had left at home, he had only one wish now – to share this news with Nan. The glee of gossip. *Schadenfreude!* He looked round at the three faces gazing at the box. He didn't want to talk to them. He wanted to talk to Nan, the only person in the world, it seemed, who knew his language.

It always took three or four pints for the 'earlies' to be able to loosen their tongues. And the 'earlies' usually went home for their tea, sometimes not emerging till the following day. The ten-to-half-past-ten drinkers had had their tea and they stayed, of course, till closing time.

But Jim realised that the silence was not the normal lack-lustre six-to-eight hush, a communal soul in a moribund state, but deliberate. Yes, deliberate, and he was the cause. Ever since he, Jim, had asked about Raphael, they had clammed up. The blow-in must be left in the dark, and not because he'd blab outside the parish, but because he didn't deserve to share the excitement. After all, he wanted to shout, I've had the baptism of twelve winters. But what was that compared with twelve generations?

He kept glancing round at the door. Hoping. Hoping. Surely Swann had gone home long ago. He imagined them by the fire in their overcrowded sitting room, while Angela knelt in the grate, trying to encourage more heat from the chimney. She'd either be blowing on the embers or playing with the tongs, redistributing the coals and the logs. Did they even know about Gilsenan? That was a thought. But of course they must. Such a gruesome event could not be hidden for more than twenty minutes in the parish.

Then Nan's at home alone. My God! Alone! He shouted at Matt for another whiskey. Nan is a shooting star that might suddenly fly out of orbit. Out of his orbit. And it would be his fault. It wasn't Nan's fault that things were different thirty years ago. What option had she but to hide the birth away, to pretend it had never happened?

'Give me change for the phone,' he shouted again. The three men squinted at him. 'Please.'

Matt pulled the pint, looked at Jim, his eyebrows cocked. 'The missus away again?'

'She's around.'

Pat Mullen swayed at his elbow. 'She's gone again.'

Jim didn't know to whom Pat referred. He dialled, scattering ten-penny pieces on the floor. He heard the unanswered buzz. He put the receiver back and began again. Perhaps he'd dialled the wrong number. The men were engrossed in the soap opera that came on every night after the news. Still no reply. Dear Jesus, Nan, please answer. Eventually he clamped back the receiver and returned to the bar stool.

And there she was. Walking into the bar. Ignoring him.

With her entry, every vestige of hope at reconciliation was wrested from him. His recent desire to hug her and ask forgiveness evaporated. Once again they took up their stances at opposite ends of the battlefield. He pretended not to see her, as she did also.

'You're looking well,' Pat offered.

Nan, conscious of her swollen eyes, turned away.

Silence settled down again. But unable to resist reactions from his customers, Matt told her of Gilsenan's untimely demise.

'My God.' She turned, in spite of herself, to him. 'Jim, did you know that?'

'It's all we've been talking about,' he lied.

Could the ice melt? Could the possibility of their having been a murder in the locality act as a catalyst to bring them back together again? He agreed it was a shock.

'But how?' Nan pursued.

'He fell in the ditch going home from the pub. And froze to death.'

She shivered. 'Poor man. Was he found face down?'

The question made people want to laugh, but they were afraid to.

'He was with Pat here till four. Isn't that right, Pat?'

'That's right.' Pat seemed still drunk, although he had only just arrived.

'And did you finish the bottle of whiskey between you?'

Jim was so pleased to be talking about this again. He tried to make it as interesting as possible. Turn it into something which had no connection with their own predicament. He moved over to be beside her. He whispered that it might not have been an accident. She nodded but turned away again.

He wanted to fix Nan in this pattern of gossip, feed her with gory details, but of course everything had to be couched in innuendo and euphemism. He imagined the excitement of murder trials and the local gardai, with their speeches delivered in convoluted police-spic. And Raphael in the dock. Raphael, for all his surliness, could stand huge and handsome in those circumstances. And the jury, townees mostly, would be impressed by this man of the soil. But even so, no matter what their opinion, the judge would advise them on his innocence.

And he'd walk out proud and free. But ... Would his back become more hunched, his splendid brown eyes more furtive? Would he hurry into the barn at night, the beam of his flash lamp scouring every nook and cranny?

But to tell the truth, Jim couldn't give a shit about the outcome of the Gilsenan incident. The only thing that mattered now was Nan. He had drunk too fast and too much. He would slow down, choose his words with care.

He tried to pick up the conversation, turning to Pat for help. The cold in the pub and out of it, the efficacy of smokeless coal, the gestation period of cows. All important topics, not to be dealt with lightly. Pat Mullen, a man who, beneath his drunken exterior, had supreme knowledge of the beef market, was of the opinion that Jim should bring his heifers to the bull as soon as possible. Otherwise the new calves would be behind for next year's autumn market.

Nan knew that Jim would find it hard to send his pets to the mincer in the sky when the time came. She foresaw having huge herds of cattle eventually and not enough land to entertain them. She suddenly realised she was thinking of the future together as a real probability, something that afternoon she thought they had written off.

She looked at Jim, his face open for a change, amiably chatting to Pat. But how would she tell him tonight that she had written to Charles to say OK, they could have him for a fortnight. How, dear God, how? But she hadn't posted the letter. There was still time to tear it up. She turned from them again, bewildered. She drank her drink quickly and left the pub.

Jim watched her go. The momentary hiatus between them withered away. He turned to Pat again, but the latter had sunk his head in his collar. The previous hours' excitement dried up like a puddle in a hot day, the silence and sadness of winter settling back on the faces of the others.

And then closing time and please can we have another no certainly not would you give us a break. And no Gilsenans to be seen and only one left anyway.

Nan, sober and guarded, hung around the kitchen till Jim came home. She dithered about with hot drinks and biscuits, opening and shutting cupboard doors, occasionally looking over at him, feeling again that lack of permanence as though, in spite of her seeming anchorage, she was only passing through. Is it the having of children, then, the only thing that fixes the human in space? And yet they were both threatened, because until now their friendship, love even, had been cemented by their individual freedom.

She knew she had to post the letter.

'So. You're inviting this man here? And when? And do I have no say about whom you invite to my house, our house?'

'I would have told you the other night, only you were drunk.' Jim looked at his wife, that Goyaesque figure with the Sephardic genes, with this history that he'd known nothing about a few months ago. Her thick dark hair scraped off her forehead accentuated her worst features, her wide cheeks, her thick lips. He had no more to say to her. He went out into the thin air, the grey December day, to talk to his animals. With them he was safe. He humped the bale of hay through the gate and watched the heifers nosing and burrowing into it.

And Nan watched *him* as he leant over the gate, thinking she'd never seen a man looking less like a farmer, ill-clad, skinny, hungover, with his unsuitable trousers rattling in the wind, his sparse hair standing up like tin tacks above his domed brow, which was pink with the cold, and her heart was scalded with pity and love in the same way as when she had watched

Charles walking down that terrible road into that terrible house.

But how can this be? How feel pity and love for strangers especially this man with whom she'd lived for over twenty years, who'd suddenly become a different being, a creature quite removed from all their past intimacies, their laughter, their teasing, their trust?

Can a relationship end as easily as if you had thrown an electric switch? Snap! Everything wiped out, like rain on the windscreen of a car.

And what did her son want from her anyway? Love? Hatred? Revenge? Or does he really seek friendship? She felt drained. As if her skin had tightened, as if her whole body had become desensitised.

She turned from the window and went into her room. She sat down at the piano but didn't open the lid. Would she ever open the lid again? Had she thrown a switch on her career as well? Was she, Nan, healthy, eclectic, talented, about to throw everything over because she was too selfish to say, 'No.'

Yet such are the habits of long association, they both went to Rogan's that night as though everything was the same as ever.

They rang the Swanns, who joined them. Nick was hiding under an 'old boy' attitude and Angela, having lost her summer tan was shivery, wrapped up in layers of garments. The four people traded banalities, drank fast, and Christmas hovered over them a fortnight away. And none of them, mentioned the imminence of Charles's arrival. Yet it sat like a bird on all their shoulders.

Three-quarters of the way through the evening, the Swanns went home, muttering about their daughters, something about driving them somewhere. Which left Nan and Jim with nothing to say, sitting awkwardly near each other on their sloping bus seats.

After a few minutes Jim said, 'Excuse me,' and went in the direction of the Gents.

Time passed. Matt was shouting last orders.

'Where's Jim?' she asked Fonsie Slater who was sitting next to her.

'Haven't a clue.'

As the hedgerows flashed past, Jim patted his pocket to make sure he had his credit cards and loose cash. He would stop at a B&B and in the morning make some decision about his next move. One thing he was determined on was not to have to meet this Charles person. Ever. He felt guilty for having the car, knowing what Nan was like without wheels. She'd have to rent one. She could well afford it.

His thoughts were veering in a direction foreign to him. Bitterness, a penumbra he couldn't shake off. Time after time he asked himself what did it matter if Nan paid attention to this person, it would only be for a short time, but he'd immediately fall back into his old angry tracks of how dare she without asking his permission?

After a couple of hours realising he'd soon be in Belfast and that he must find a place to stay before he was in the city, he was flagged down by an RUC man asking for identity. And where was he going? To Belfast. He waved him on and Jim felt his legs a little weak after the encounter. He decided he wanted to pee and pulled in a few hundred yards from the checkpoint. The effect of the few pints he'd had in Rogan's had worn off and he began to feel sober and stupid. The cold made him shake as the pee trickled into the hard shoulder of the road. What the fuck was he doing in this no man's land when his nice warm bed was waiting for him at home? He turned the car and headed back the way he'd come. The road, empty enough at this time of night, unpeeled mile after mile of boring similarity. The glow from his headlights occasionally lit up the eyes of some feral creature, a weasel or more likely a cat. Until the rain came down in sheets and he had to concentrate on maintaining his vision. When off the highway and back on the familiar pothole-avoiding roads, he talked loudly to himself: 'I'll go, fuck it, and fuck her too and her English son. Yes, to Australia or some God damn fucking place. I'll go and then she can scream and rant for her lost protector. And seemingly this English person isn't that friendly and only wants to get back at her dumping him in his English garden . . .' And before he knew where he was he was seated in his parked car with the gloomy vista of an unlit house, his mind blocked with bitterness, while underneath his body yearned to climb in beside her and hold her and hold her and hold her.

Nan had run out into the night when she realised Jim must have driven off. But the dry rectangle left where the car had been seemed the final stupidity at the end of a stupid day. Fonsie Slater, with his bucktooth grin, was an insult to humanity. Trust her to end up with him on this fractured evening. What did Jim imagine he was at? He'll probably crash and kill himself. And so what? He's nothing but a pain in the neck these last weeks. Anyone would think she'd acquired a toy boy and was off on a sexual odyssey instead of the quagmire of emotional disorder in which she foundered. Jesus. What a fucking bastard. And she'd now no car. No car and Charles arriving tomorrow. What in the name of fucking Jesus would she do?

And here she was, stuck beside Fonsie and no way of getting home. Raphael had been missing since the accident, so there was no four-wheel drive to ride home in. Raphael might be a murderer but he was a decent man when it came to lifts.

Two weeks before Christmas. That meant they'd have to stay at home for the holiday. Would they be able to shift Charles before that? Unlikely. So that was his plan. She ordered another hot whiskey and took one of Fonsie's proffered cigarettes. She had a mind to ask Fonsie did he like Christmas, because nobody ever admitted that they liked Christmas. A waste of time and money and the pubs were shut.

'Do you like Christmas?' Fonsie said.

Nan laughed. 'It's on my mind.'

'It's a cunt of a time,' Fonsie said, 'a real cunt.'

'Indeed.' She looked into his washed-out eyes. He had pale eyebrows, as though they were dusted with cement or dried concrete. In fact the whole face had a sandy look. Shaving must be painful. 'Will your mother not cook the turkey?' She imagined Onion-head slurping his food down while Maggie Slater waited on the two of them. 'Will your sister come home for the holiday?' There was an inevitable sister in England.

'She has her own family over there.' Fonsie looked uncomfortable about giving away so much personal information.

'So you have nephews and nieces?' Nan was relentless.

'Aye.' Fonsie rose and went into the front bar. Enough was enough.

She could hear the rain crashing on the flat roof above the toilet when she went for a pee. What a scumbag to leave her like this.

It was Matt Rogan himself who eventually took her home. She had considered ringing the Swanns, but she felt she had already involved Nick in enough of her troubles.

Later she sat in the cold empty kitchen, contemplating a damp patch over the window. She wondered if Charles was any good at fixing things. The gutter needed seeing to. Not really an impossible job, but then Jim was afraid of heights.

At one o'clock she went up to bed and lay curled and sleepless. She dozed and dreamt and woke with a start when she heard the car. It was five o'clock on a dark winter morning. She could feel the cold running like water up her arm when she lifted it over the duvet. She listened for any sound that might indicate his plans. She had to admit she was relieved he was back. Dear God, in such a crazy mood he could easily have crashed the car.

At length – what on earth was he doing? – she heard the footsteps. She dived under the covers and shut her eyes tight. 'I'm putting out the light, Dada,' she used to call when Louis Wine fussed about her reading in bed, as she listened to him fidgeting in the parlour before he finally climbed the stairs. And when he was safely in his bedroom, she'd put the light on again to go back to her book. How wonderful to be curled up under the blankets – no duvets in those days – with the book at an angle and the lamp slanting down over her shoulder.

But now Jim was in the room. She felt the bed sag as he climbed in. She longed to turn to him, her arms aching to pull him round, the blood rushing to her throat, but she couldn't cope with his refusals any more.

He must have driven for miles before he realised the futility of it. She gave a little sigh, hoping he might acknowledge her need for him. But he lay there with his back to her till he eventually fell asleep.

She was up at a reasonable hour but Jim slept on. She had to be at Knock by three o'clock. (She had decided to meet him after all.) It was nearly one when Jim emerged, looking hang-dog. He still seemed confused, unable to meet her eye. When he fiddled around with the coffee pot he said, 'I'm thinking of going back to college to study anthropology.'

'What gave you that notion?'

'I'm in a rut. There's nothing more to find in this shagging country.'

'I'll have to leave in half an hour.'

Jim busied himself rinsing the pot and spooning coffee into it. 'Also it would take me to distant countries. There's far more to undiscovered human remains than boring artefacts and burial tombs.' He poured the boiling water into the pot, got a cup and sat himself down.

'What about me?'

Jim waved his hand in an arc as he tilted his chair to reach into the fridge for the milk.

'Oh, God, Jim, can we not have peace for the rest of the day?'

'There's petrol in the car.'

On the journey back from Knock the rain pelted down. Charles mentioned the weather, in fact. And Nan dodged articulated trucks and darkness fell. The road smudged by desultory bungalows, throwing beams of light on to their forecourts, brought a comment from him. 'Not like England.' Where, he said, people generally don't live on the side of the road. She would have liked to go into an explanation for the phenomenon, tell how thirty years ago the same people would have been living in isolation up unimaginable boreens and with the new rise in living standards had built themselves houses nearer to 'civilisation'. So the silences lengthened and by the time they got home Nan was exhausted and edgy.

The size of Charles's suitcase was ominous. He peeled off his expensive Parka and looked round for somewhere to hang it. Nan, determined not to act the fussy mother, ignored this and went to make tea and put out biscuits. She wanted to please him, to make him feel he was home, to show off her native hospitality so he would get to like Ireland, the place, after all, of his ancestors. If only Jim ... The thought was not worth pursuing.

Should she pretend that her husband would soon be here to make the dinner? Or should she tell him that Jim wouldn't leave the pub till closing time, drunk and obnoxious? But instead, 'When you've had a cup of tea I'll show you round.'

He sniffed around the kitchen, a dog marking his new territory, then sat abruptly and poured his tea. Nan felt that at any moment she would start apologising. For the unreliable central heating, the spareness of the kitchen, the remoteness of the house, the darkness, the weeping winter that would continue to do so for the next six months. But why should she? She loved this place as passionately as Jim. They had their own style, each their own rooms the way they liked it. So again the unspoken sentences hummed around them and Charles munched on a ginger biscuit.

At length she decided she'd take him to town to the new fish restaurant in High Street. Show him they were as modern as Crowsfort.

She brought him to his room, which she had prettied up with a paper shade on the bedside lamp, a new duvet with a striped cotton cover, a small bookshelf filled with books. It had life. One large window faced out into the blackness of the night. 'You have a nice view,' she laughed. 'In the daytime.'

Going to the car, she knew that the only way to ease her tension was to talk. Talk about anything, but talk. So she started off by telling him that normally Jim cooked the evening meal but he was 'out' tonight. 'He's thinking of going back to university to study anthropology. He is of course a learned archaeologist, but of course as you probably know Ireland is immensely rich in prehistoric tombs and artefacts, but most of them have been excavated or listed. He thinks that a new field of study would be beneficial.' How much more rubbish could she throw at him when Jim – if they ever met – would probably be his most determinedly earthy, non-cultured self, and engage him in discussions about animals and potato blight. Probably throw in the famine in order to point out Charles's ignorance of Irish history. But she could go on like this for hours. While they drove to town, while they ate in the restaurant, while they drank their wine, while they returned and she put him to bed, read him a story and tucked him up. Just to drone on and on for weeks while Jim slept, snarled and went to the pub.

And she had not apologised for anything, although she'd been conscious of all the house's shortcomings. A wall needing paint, a hinge on the bathroom door half broken, a window that was jammed, not to mention the singing cistern, and on the way down she'd brought him into her study, run her hand over the shiny lid of her piano and said, 'This, at least, is perfect.'

In the restaurant, Charles said he hated pizzas.

'So do I!' Nan looked seriously at him.

'The fish here is good.' So she suggested he start with the fish platter.

He shrugged. 'OK, Ma!' A half-smile pitted his cheek. He had small, uneven but super-white teeth.

She said, 'I think –'

'I know what you're going to say: Don't call me Ma.'

'It's unreal. I'm unreal.' She took the menu from him. 'Try the monkfish, it's reliable.'

She wouldn't talk any more, not make up any more sentences, sentences with clauses and sub-clauses. They would eat in silence. 'OK, Ma.' Is that all he'd said all evening? He had nodded and shrugged and hummed while all the time his angry eyes had searched her face, her person. Little circles of fear ran through her. Was his hatred enough to make him want to kill her? She ordered a bottle of red wine. Spanish Rioja.

There. Let the space between us be.

They ate. Drained the bottle, ordered another. Then he suddenly leant towards her. 'Nan,' he said, 'it is not.'

'Not what?' She tried to edge away. Was it the wine, she wondered.

The waiter came back and stood over their table. 'Anything else, Madam?' She shook her head. He retreated into the kitchen. They started on the second bottle and Charles began.

★

'I'm a shit,' Jim told Pat Mullen, who swayed at his side.

'Huh?'

'Yes.'

'It's nice to be nice.'

'It's nice to be a shit.'

Pat tossed his pink head and laughed. The laugh, nearly silent, went in and out of his chest in short jerks. 'Where's Nan?'

'That's it.' Jim reached to the counter. 'Two pints, please.'

'Stout?'

Jim nodded. When Pat got drunk he'd order neat gin and pour it into his pint.

'Cancer of the liver,' he said.

'Not surprising.'

'Have you got it?' He asked this as though he'd thrown him a ball and Jim had caught it.

'Not's I know it.'

Pat swayed, silently wondering about this.

'We're all afraid of cancer,' Jim said, 'but there are lots worse diseases going the road.'

'What are they?'

'Well, AIDS for one.'

'That's from too much sex,' Pat said.

'Not enough, maybe.'

Pat gave his in-and-out laugh. Jim looked closely at Pat, the forty-five-year-old orphan swaying beside him. Had he ever been with a woman? Sometimes, when amused, Pat gave frisky little jumps, to accompany his laugh. This he did now and Jim wanted to hug him. But such a thing in Rogan's was unthinkable. Mind you, it had been rumoured that Matt Rogan had brought his dick to big Jack the postman for a rub. But strictly behind doors. Jack had marvelled at its size, but told Matt to put it away.

Greta came in, accompanied by an unknown teenager, and they both turned their attention on her.

'You're looking well,' Pat said.

Greta had a rich crop of red hair which sent the boys mad. It made them want to nest in it. Otherwise she couldn't boast much of a face. There were others far prettier than she was, but she just oozed a fatal whatever it is – are there names for it? – that left a trail of unconsummated pricks behind her. And neither Jim nor Pat was unaware of this. As she passed them the expressions on their faces underwent a change. The skin around their cheeks became tighter, their eyes took on a misty vagueness and each immediately forgot what the other had been saying. Jim, feeling he had lost every vestige of security, wanted to weep on Pat's shoulder, and he began to do so in his imagination. Confused and drunk, he remained thus, his secret self racked with sobs until Matt Rogan intervened: 'We can't have this carry-on in the pub. You can do it outside.'

'You must go outside to shit or pee or make love or weep,' he told Pat.

They had both been looking at the ground for the last while, Jim's burst of imagined weeping having subsided. Pat rocked in agreement.

'The public must be sealed off from all bodily excretions.' Pat again rocked.

'Do you think it's the fault of the Church?'

'Did you ever ride a donkey?' Pat asked.

Jim wondered why Nan hadn't rung the pub. He already regretted his rudeness earlier and wished she'd ring. But if she did, would he react the same way? Nowadays he never knew what he'd do next.

'Did you ever go to the market and sell cheap by mistake?'

Pat turned curiously on Jim. This was a real conversation and worthy of note. He thought about it. Greta laughed in the distance. She had a greedy laugh, Jim pitied the teenager. He wondered where she'd found him. In town probably. Little did he know. Meanwhile, Pat was deep in wonder.

He remembered the most recent mart had been disappointing. But it hadn't been his fault. Everyone was in the same boat with the BSE.

'I must must must,' Jim said.

'Huh?'

'Sorry, I was talking to myself. Anyway I'm sure you never did.'

'You have to sometimes.' Pat finally answered Jim's question.

'But not through prevarication. Necessity,' Jim suggested.

Matt was shouting and turning on and off the lights. It was twelve fifteen. 'The guards,' he muttered. The guards hadn't been seen for weeks. It was a feeble ploy which seldom worked. There was a smug row of three-quarters full pints on the counter, but as usual Jim had left it late to order his last pint. He noticed, however, that Pat had sneaked up to the counter unbeknownst to himself and had a full pint balanced on the shelf.

'Can I have a short?'

'No way,' Matt said, pulling in the empty glasses and lighting a cigarette.

Matt's wife, Fiona, was an easier touch, but she was also adamant. Another thing, he'd have to walk home or wait till Matt had cleared up. But he didn't care. It was a dry night for once. A freezing moon hung in the sky. He began to sing.

> Love is teasing and love is easing
> And love's a pleasure when first it's new.
> But when you grow older, love grows colder
> And fades away like the morning dew.

'Not true,' he shouted, as the last line fell out of him. 'And they've stolen my house,' he told the bar, but no one was interested. 'That's it.'

The road was white with moonlight and his shadow walked behind him. It was a calm, frosty night. One of Pat's cows mooed and he mooed back. He walked straight and tall and then he danced a little to his own humming. 'I'll dance the last dance with you,' he told the hedge. 'But I won't fall in the sheuch. No. Not like Marty Gilsenan. No. Not Jim McDonald.' He stopped dancing. He was afraid he'd meet the ghost that haunted hereabouts. He hurried on.

Not a light in the house. The shagging car parked neat as a matchbox. Jim tripped. 'Fuck fuck fuck. And fuck.' The moon hidden now behind the house was no help. They'd built the house the wrong way round. The Irish are funny like that. No foresight. Something to do with the famine. Made us wary. And cynical. It's like that with blackberries. Or watercress. But we eat lots of garlic. Jim heard his voice nattering away. He remembered old Gilsenan, before he'd passed away, saying, 'I've a lovely house,' as though he were about to burst into tears. And then what happened? No wonder he whined. We should get J.B. Keane down here to write about it. Make a great film. And they could throw his and Nan's problems in for good measure. The country's gone to hell altogether. My God, he suddenly remembered that this Charles person must be somewhere. Polluting the spare room, he supposed. Unless in Nan's bed. The kitchen was freezing. No him to light the stove and the fucker's gone out. What a crowd of tooremelauns, useless, probably never seen a real fire. Probably had gas fires built into the grate with false flames. Oh, yes. He knew the kind of thing. All neat and tidy like. The kind you can't throw cigarettes into. And fuck, he'd forgotten to buy some in the pub. What sort of an eejit was he? 'Love is teasing and love is easing.' He rummaged around for a packet of roll-up tobacco. He pulled the drawer out of the kitchen table and it fell on the floor, scattering its contents, half empty seed packets, a pliers, two round, yoked, three-pronged plugs and a miscellany of nails and screws and washers which he had put in a jam jar. The jar had broken and the contents were strewn on the floor. Jee sus. He knelt down and started gathering everything up and putting it back in the drawer, which he stuffed back into its place . . . and of course no tobacco. 'Greta's a sexy get. But don't tell Nan.' And there was Nan in the doorway in her dressing gown, saying, 'What's going on? The place is crashing about our ears.'

'Ha ha. So it is.'

'You are pissed. You are fucking pissed.' She turned round and shouted, 'Every fucking night of the week. You can sleep in the sitting room.'

As if she'd never been pissed in her life! The fucking bitch. What was she trying to prove? 'Love is teasing and love is easing and love's a pleasure when first it's new, you old bitch,' and he burst into tears. He howled like he'd howled in his imagination in the pub. He laid his head on the table and his body heaved and bucked as he cried out to the empty room, 'You don't love me, you bitch, you never loved me, you just used me as a crutch so that you could travel the world on that ebony beast. And now are you happy? You've got a ready-made son without having the trouble to bring him up and you can throw me off like a worn coat. Give me to the St Vincent de Paul shop or the Cerebral Palsy. Fuck it fuck it fuck it.'

'At five I was sent to a primary school in Hindhead, but, you see, I was prissied up, not like the other kids – I was fair game. They did what they liked with me. Of course, I remember before that. In fact my fourth birthday on a train going somewhere and my mother had a cake for me which broke all over the floor of the carriage and both my parents flew into a rage. Blaming each other and, of course, I took the opportunity to bawl my eyes out until all hell let loose and the train might as well have ground to a halt and thrown us out. But it carried on, chuff chuff chuff. But to go back to my school, that was the worst day of my life. My first day at school. Both my parents drove me there – Father must have taken the morning off, because normally it was only Mother who drove me – and they just dumped me. I kept screaming and clinging on to my mother. I tore her dress, I remember, and she said mildly, "Naughty." That was all she ever said. "Naughty" and sometimes, "Naughty, naughty." I learned at a very early age that I could get away with anything. I could throw tantrums and break the china and she'd say, "Naughty." Or, "Now Mother is very cross," and Father would rage at her that she was making me into a ninny and that he'd toughen me up. But luckily he forgot about this immediately afterwards, because he was always in a hurry to go to his golf. Then when he'd gone, Mother would take me on her knee and say how much she hated golf – the game, the people, the pavilion, the golf clubs, the golf balls full of gutta-percha. And I thought of gutta-percha as somewhere where birds sat on the roof, and I snuffled into her blouse and bit the pearls which she wore "because they had been a present from Dad when we were happy". And this satisfied me, because then I'd have her to myself because they didn't like each other any more.

'Well, school. I suppose you want to hear that I was a scholar, but you'll be disappointed. I was lazy and never listened to the teacher. I couldn't wait to get home to eat all the cakes and goodies she'd have for me. Also to get away from the bullying brutes that passed as children, with their hefty shoulders and huge feet.

'And I couldn't admit to Mother that I was being terrorised, because she'd have gone to the headmaster and that would have been the end of me. They'd have killed me probably. So I had to put up with the taunting and torture they invented for me every day. I often thought of running away with the half-crown or whatever. I'd heard of boys who ran away to London and were just another missing person. A name on a file. I liked that idea. I suppose it was one of the reasons I decided to look for you, because I was a name on a file, and worth a bit of research. Anyway, I began to hate my parents. I hated them because they sent me to this torture chamber every day. But at last it ended. I got the eleven-plus by the skin of my teeth and was sent to a grammar school not far from home. And that was the beginning of a new series of disasters. Disasters not actually connected with my going to school but coinciding with it. Mother took me aside one day and said she was planning to run away with me, because Dad had betrayed her confidence. He had told the deputy headmaster that I had bad blood. My God, I tell you, that gave me a fright. I was always poking into books and one day I came across a pocket medical dictionary, where I looked up all the blood diseases – anaemia, leukaemia, rare conditions like haemophilia and God knows what. And what you ate clogged up your arteries and your heart got affected. Cholesterol was the danger, I learned. From then on I was obsessed with my health. I refused to eat all the rich food she stuffed me with, cakes and sausages and so on, so I got very thin and peaky. The doctor was consulted and he recommended a no-nonsense approach. Millions were starving all over the world and I was just an impossible being that had no right to any human kindness. And that my mother was kindness itself, he had never known a more caring mother. And that because I was an only child I must be spoilt rotten. Of course, he didn't actually say that, but inferred it was basically my mother's fault and that she mustn't listen to me. "But what about my blood?" I piped in, which made them go into peels of laughter. "It's not funny," I said. "Dad says I've bad blood." The doctor looked at my mother with a crook in his eyebrows and mother gave a mysterious shake of the head. In fact her whole body swayed as though she were on a swivel chair. I realised then that there was something sinister going on which I must get to the bottom of. I consulted a boy of my age, Gerald his name was – we were in our second year at the grammar school – and he promised he would look into it for me. I said it was urgent, because the doctor and my mother were plotting something and it might be to my detriment. I felt I was in danger. I became paranoid, always looking at my veins, pressing my wrists and my ankles, my body bent at an angle over my desk. The teachers lost patience with me never paying attention, my marks got worse and worse. I use to copy Gerald's maths every morning. I had to pay him most of my pocket money to get in early. And Gerald was no further in his researches. He said he had heard one of his uncles say about a neighbour that he had bad blood because he was Irish. And he'd asked his uncle what he'd meant, but all the uncle had said was that he didn't mean to be racist, which made him think that perhaps he meant that there was some African blood in his veins because they were always going on about racism and how they mustn't be racist but it was the blacks at the end of the road they alluded to. By the time I was fifteen and going on for my O levels I had what you would call a nervous breakdown . . . I started to duplicate everything in the room. I used to stare and stare, trying to get things back to normal. But the walls and desks wouldn't stay still. One day, it was in the French class, my mother suddenly appeared. She went straight to the teacher and they both nodded silently and then she marched over to me and told me she was taking me home. She swayed in front of my eyes. "What is it?" I tried to control my voice which had a flutey squeak to it. She didn't answer, so I followed her shakily. My legs felt as though they hung out of my torso and it was all I could do to stay upright. In the car I lay back into the seat and shut my eyes. It felt better that way, I thought, until the light began to trick my eyelids and I fancied that all my bad blood was pouring out of my head and streaming down my face. I clapped both my hands on my cheeks to feel the ooze, but they were dry. If I held them there, then, I thought I'd be safe. I think I slept, because the next thing I knew was that there was a woman in white bending over me with a syringe and I was in bed. Everything was suddenly clear. I sat up in terror. Because I'd watched plenty of horror movies where the enemy gave you an injection, which turned you into a vegetable. "Please don't," I screamed. The woman had biceps like a weightlifter's and she took a good hold of me. I was weak from starvation, thin and weedy, no match for this Amazonian creature. Before she gave me the jab, I wondered where my mother had got to and what she was thinking of, leaving me in this new torture chamber. Ever since I was four I'd been sent to one torture chamber after another, but this was undoubtedly the worst. It must have been about forty-eight hours later when I woke to find a new nurse holding a tray over my head. "Now, now," she said, "din-dins."

'I sat up. I felt fine and very hungry. The walls were no longer closing in on me. She placed a bed rest over my covers with the tray on it. There was watery scrambled egg on damp toast and a pot of tea, with milk and sugar. Manna. I ate – or drank – the lot. Now, I thought, sooner or later I'll get the answer to my problem. Nurses are a pushover, Gerald had told me. Yes.

'When I found out the real reason for my father's criticism I saw daylight for the first time. As though I'd been walking around with a blanket over my head, fumbling about, poking here and there, trying to get my balance in a landslide, and now the ground had steadied. I demanded to see my father. At first the nurses shook their heads, crooking their eyebrows at each other. But I insisted, pretending that I missed him and that I'd get better if he visited me. At last they agreed to send for him. When he came he wouldn't look at me. He stood near the window – which, incidentally, looked out on a high wall.

'"Where's mother?"

'"She's too busy to come."

'More lies.

'"Never mind," I said. "I don't care if I'm not your real child. In fact I'm pleased."

'He rocked back on his heels as though in an underground train.

'"You've been a disappointment to us."

'"I know."

'"You see, son."

'"Don't"

'"Well, we intended to tell you very early on – the psychiatrist told us to – but time sort of passed."

'He was wilting away before my very eyes, my tough golf-playing father, the company surveyor who had passed all his exams, who had pulled himself up by his bootstraps and married a very refined lady – my mother – who came from a solid yeoman family in the north of England, and whom everyone respected and admired for her maternal rectitude, and her wifely skills, who never wanted to better herself but believed her place was with the family, and who had a solid house in a solid village in a solid south-eastern county and built walls of respectability around it, a little citadel of fraudulence.

'Four days later, I said to my mother, who had at last come to see me, "Ask the nurse for my clothes. I'm going home." I jumped out of bed. "You can tell her the cause of my break-down and that I'm cured."'

Nan went over to pay the bill.

'It's all right,' Charles, at her elbow, said. 'You paid for the dinner in Crowsfort.'

They drove for a mile or two until Nan, dragging at her seat belt, looked round at him. 'That,' she said, 'was tough,' and after another few silent miles, said, 'You'd have been no better off with me,' and again after more miles said, 'They must have meant well. Just didn't know.'

And it's the 'just don't knows', she supposed, that do the damage. And the 'just don't knows' lurk in every crevice, every nook and cranny, of the planet, doing damage. And was she one of them too, who, by handing this person over to such a well-got, well-meaning couple, did irreparable damage, because she just didn't know?

She dried up, her muttering in the car stopped. He had thrown down the gauntlet and she couldn't pick it up.

Their house was as cold and draughty as a sieve. It was after twelve and she must hustle Charles to bed before Jim returned.

Elsie, what will I do? Nan tossed, punched the pillows, tried to read, to slur her eyes into sleepiness but every so often she shot up in bed to listen for the crashes and curses.

And they began around one fifteen. The cursing and one almighty crash followed by further wails of misery. God bring me sleep. Dear Jewish God, Jehovah of my father, bring me sleep. And again she was back in that hostel, playing 'Grandpa Spells' and Elsie dancing, and they'd sing, and Elsie squealing, 'Give me the Platters. Gee, I'm the Great Pretender, pretending that I'm not alone.' And they'd hug till Miss Charity brought all hell on their heads. And she handed him over in his 'blue-for-a-boy' clothes. And now he slept in his bed, all prettied up like a cottage tea room.

God, the noise! She leapt up and threw on her dressing gown, and there in the kitchen was Jim on his knees, scratching about like an old cockerel pecking for seed.

Jim fell twice before making it to the bed and Nan thought, I'll change Charles's name back to Séan. She let Jim paw her breasts, half aware of it, so tense was she, and thinking that if she did it could swing the balance one way or another. When Jim started to gnaw at her nipples she said, 'You don't give two fucks about me, you just want a poke. And you wouldn't get it up anyway.' Furious, she turned her back on him. Nothing was working out any more.

And still sleep evaded her. Sleep, my sister, please wrap me up. And she thought then of her sister, who had suddenly got cancer of the throat at the age of thirty-nine, and how small and precious was the memory of that day in the rain as they had stood outside the chapel in the street, in Westmeath, with her husband, holding the two daughters, one in each hand, his stone grey eyes and Meath face wide with incomprehension. Her two brothers, late and puffing, disgorged themselves from their car like crooks in a Hollywood movie and reassembled themselves near the hearse. The eldest, Samuel, was also the tallest and Nan, who had always found him remote and unforthcoming, was now surprised to see two tears glistening in the hollow beneath his eyes. At first she had thought it was rain, for it was ready to spill over when it had collected in the brim of his grey trilby, but when she realised how sad he was it increased her own wretchedness. She had moved nearer to him and lain her hand on his sleeve, feeling the wet wool of his Crombie between her cold fingers, a reminder of birthday parties in the parlour and how she had always tried to drag him into their childish games among the sombre mahogany furniture. And how none of them knew of her dark secret that day. That she had brought home from England and would forever lie hidden in the cells of her brain. How they had silently followed the mutes into the church and taken their places in the front pew, Lizzie's husband and her two nieces nearest the aisle, so that they could go to the altar rail first.

It was as if he hadn't told his story. Or half his story. He'd said nothing about earaches, running noses, scuffed knees, night terrors. He'd given her a précis. And she would fill in the details. Day after day. Small details would come to mind. His father with his golf-playing shoulders, his mother in neat cardigan suits, white shirts with bow ties, like the woman in the Wheatsheaf. Her superiority to his father, her sniffs of displeasure. Her barrenness a constant source of amazement. Luck, even. As it stopped him forcing her to have sex. He might even have had a scrubby little mistress in the office, whom he quickly fucked under the desk, their feet rustling the wastepaper basket, the phone off the hook. How he would come home and turn on the black and white telly and send Charles off to bed, and Charles, his meagre frame under shorts and jersey, would stand hopefully looking at his mother, who'd say, 'Do as your father tells you.'

She lit the range, which had gone out, and in the dim light went to prepare some breakfast. The two men still slept. Soon they would surely meet, but what did Charles know of *her*? She would never précis the intervening years. Because parents don't have a past. Parents don't have feelings, except towards the children, and they are always wrong. Their emotions are a list with little ticks. Overprotective. Too casual. Neglectful. Cruel. They don't have talents or ambitions. They are cooks and cleaners. Mothers are bad drivers . . .

Charles came in sideways, dressed as for the street. His handsome features clean and shaved. Was he better or worse for having shouldered off some of his self-pity? But not his anger. No, his tones had been neutral as his story unfolded. Ironic, even. Yes. Directed at her. 'See what you did to me.'

And God, he was beautiful. His beauty sent ripples up her spine. He was as tall as Jim, but unlike Jim, whose body most mornings resembled that of a refugee who had lost his passport, Charles's frame seemed fixed in a nimbus of security. Superiority, even . . . Imbued in him, perhaps, by his English upbringing.

They both had the pointed features that pleased her. But there the resemblance ended. Charles was much fairer. His chestnut hair swung back from his forehead, deep curls fanning the tips of his ears, revealing a clear brow, and those dark blue eyes, large and round as wild plums. Yes. She had borne in her womb a beautiful . . . what? Viper? What if . . . She wondered once again what he would have been like if she'd kept him, lived sordidly, in cheap lodgings, fucking with strangers. Indeed, got 'knocked up' again, giving him a sister, sent both off to the local primary with snot in their noses and odd socks. Her career out the window. Collected the 'Unmarried Mothers' and done waitressing jobs on the sly. What would he be now? A Londoner, streetwise. And her letters home a tissue of lies.

Yes, she would have written home. She had a good job. No, she had never married. Once in a while she would have taken the mail boat home, to see her father and sister and brothers, and Charles would have been warned and bound over for some minor felony.

'Would you like an egg?' she said.

He tapped the top of his egg with a spoon, carefully peeling back the shell and she wished her father were still alive so that she could show him this grandson who peeled the eggshell in the same way that he used to.

She heard Jim on the stairs. There would be introductions. Jim, this is my son, Charles. Charles, this is my husband, Jim. She watched Jim come in and they gazed at each other like two ganders. Charles with spoon in midair, Jim with one hand on the back of a chair as he forced on a shoe with the other.

'So you are . . .' He didn't finish the sentence as he hopped across the floor, looking into Charles's face. 'So what do you think of your mother? Isn't she amazing? She's my wife, you know.' He put on his second shoe and stood up straight. 'Introduce us, Nan darling.'

She mumbled the names, thinking, he's still drunk, while he turned to rake the fire, muttering, 'Can nobody in this house do anything but me?'

Charles stirred his coffee, as though Jim hadn't spoken. Nan stared at both of them, haunted by a memory of her two brothers fighting over the wireless, one of them screaming for Radio Luxembourg, the other wanting to hear the football news, and how she had hidden under a chair to make herself invisible. And oh, how she wished, more than anything, to run to the piano, to lose herself in something trivial, go back into childhood – Liszt's piano concerto, for example – to hammer away her tensions. And she thought, Fuck them both, they are nothing to do with me. Was the blood that ran in his veins her responsibility? Or just the baggage of fate that we all store in our bodies? That he stores, and that she, in her innocence and incomprehension, had unwittingly caused.

'Your wife is a professional woman?' Charles broke the silence.

And Nan was gutted. The poor little woman needs a hobby. That's what they all think from Matt Rogan up and down, and now what Jim calls that English person thinks.

'Did your father wear bicycle clips when going to work?'

'No.'

'Did he tuck his trousers into his socks, then?'

'You know perfectly well that my father was a professional man. What are you trying to prove?'

'My grandfather was a postman,' Jim said, and broke into peels of laughter. 'What kind of a car did your father drive? A Merc? A Datsun?'

'I'll use your bathroom,' Charles said, and left the room.

Jim listened for the piano but the house had closed in its walls. He switched on the light. The debris of the previous night blazed into perspective. The odd nail lay between the flags, a piece of paper with an unknown telephone number lay face up under the table. He craned his head to read the digits but was none the wiser.

He was cycling the Killiney road to school. The rain scalded his bare legs, his long socks had concertinaed into his shoes. He met his grandfather coming from the post office. He'd done his early rounds and was on his way home for breakfast. 'Hello, Granda.' His grandfather's face was smudged with the rain, his post office cap brimming over with water. How he envied his granda, off home. He didn't have to go to school. 'Hello,

Jim.' The two bicycles passed each other and water fanned up between them.

At the school gate, his friend Seamus yelled, 'A dying duck in a thunderstorm. You'll never guess. My old man's bought a Ford 8. Lucky sucker.' His father could now drive to work instead of taking the Shankhill bus, as it happened the Wexford bus, which took the workers into town at a quarter to eight. It bowled slowly up the village, stopping twice in the process. It was his last year at National and soon he'd be on that bus, bound for Blackrock College. The little scholar.

They took off their shoes and went into class. Mr Knowles was a Scotsman who had come to Ireland during the war to avoid conscription. He wiped his long nose with his snot-green handkerchief and rolled out his series of sarcasms with which he peppered his introduction to the unwashed lower beings with whom fate had landed him. 'Now, boys, we are not here to dilly-dally.'

In spite of being Scottish, Mr Knowles hated the Irish. Because of his knowledge of Scottish Gaelic he had secured his job. And Jim knew that he secretly gloried in Cromwell's massacres. So it pleased Jim to cite incidences of his butchery, an inkling of which he gleaned from his grandfather and his readings outside class, something Mr Knowles did not encourage.

'Pity the sucker didn't stay in England to get himself butchered by the Gerries,' Seamus said at break. They had just suffered Miss Clarke's cocoa. Brown liquid with a viscous scum. If you said anything to her she bridled like a teenager, saying, 'I'm not my father's daughter for nothing.' She claimed to be Tom Clarke's daughter, but nobody believed her.

'The Irish are obstinately wild and wilfully improvident.' Jim laughed as he took a pull from the communal woodbine.

The rain had cleared by three o'clock and Jim whistled all the way home, delighted to smell the ma's baking before he opened the front door. Unfortunately the ma, like Nan's ma, had gone and died the day before his fourteenth birthday. He had tried to lie down beside her because she whispered to him that his present was on the mantelpiece. It was a book he had asked for. *The Way That I Went*, by Robert Lloyd Praeger.

He went out in the dirty weather to feed the animals. Only three young cows, now. He had sold one off in late September. And his cows were in calf. He forked down the hay with difficulty, fighting wind and hangover in equal measures. They were hock deep in mud and he vowed that not one more day would go by before he fixed the corrugated iron on the roof of the lean-to, which was the only shelter he could offer them. The hens stood in the doorway of their coup, looking out like senior citizens. He felt like teasing them by making them eat outside, but he was too soft-hearted and threw their meal into their house, thinking, Séan? He's no Séan. How was he going to get through the next week and with Christmas Day looming? He put his hand into the nesting boxes but found no eggs. God, I wouldn't lay an egg in this weather if I had a choice. He realised he was postponing the moment when he'd go back in. He stood under the spruce at the garden's edge, looking into the lighted kitchen. Charles had come back in and was at the table. He could see the sleeve of the blue-flecked tweed jacket resting its elbow on a magazine. What was he reading? Jim stood on his toes, only to be rewarded by a bucket full of rain from a wind-blown bough above him. Fuck Matt Rogan, he thought, for not opening before six o'clock. There was always the whiskey, but that meant drinking in front of this Charles person. Spears of fury shot through him.

Unable to ride the atmosphere, Nan wandered upstairs. So she has to go on living without going too far down. Last night it was far enough, right down to Lizzie's funeral. Again. With Samuel, his dark head lowered, and the two children, Deirdre and Fionnuala, standing as Jim had stood, as she had stood, watching their own mothers being lowered into the ground. Yes. That autumn day when she had not been able to cry. Had in fact felt a peculiar wonder that things could go on so normally on such a morning. How the bread van had called as usual before they left the house, and her father with his meticulous courtesy had paid him before collecting the children to walk the mile to the cemetery. And how Lizzie had cried so much their father had to lift her up and she had clung to him, soaked and snuffling. And her two brothers, gangling youths, staggering under the weight of the coffin, missing their steps, eyes scared, wanting to do the thing right.

And those strange days, weeks, that followed, when she'd creep into her father's room when he was in the shop and pull open drawers, hoping to find something that would bring her mother back – a lock of hair, an old brown photo of a pretty woman smiling into the camera. Yes. Bring her back to Lizzie, because the awful love she felt for her sister made her cling and plead. And how she longed to play the piano and they wouldn't let her. And Samuel, now. Whom she sees rarely, perhaps once every two years, his hair still strong like their father's, a white thatch, his face carved, ivory-coloured, his shirts always fresh, looking like a consultant in a major hospital. Yet happy? She doubted it. Maura, that Limerick maiden he'd so assiduously courted, his Jewish blood heavy with desire, had disappointed him. She had turned out sickly, seeming to shrink before his eyes, and his sons, Declan and Keith, had inherited none of the delicacy of their grandfather. They lounged about, their flesh spilling on to everything – chairs, car seats, girl friends. Their trousers splayed over the sofa in front of the television. So she had stopped visiting them. She was unable to follow into their minds, Maura always seeming to be in the doorway, as though uncertain that she was wanted.

So Nan had taken to staying in the kitchen, washing dishes or standing awkwardly with dish towel in hand, asking about her health, advising this or that. They could not name her trouble. ME, some said. Others, the nerves. Blood tests all showed up negative. Eventually she knew it must be Samuel's fault, but Samuel was faultless, so how explain the dilemma?

Limerick? In four weeks' time she was due in Limerick, to accompany Declan Swift on that awkward duet of Ivan Jackson's. Declan was the sweetest violinist she knew. It was a pleasure, even an honour, to play with him. But now four weeks, even four years, mightn't be long enough to master that piece. She stared at her piano, that beautiful ebony beast, Jim called it, but saw not what she should have, herself in her long satin gown, Declan in his smart waistcoat, but the ivy tapping the glass outside, with that untamed monster called winter surrounding them on all sides and two strangers somewhere in the house full of longings and twistings that she could never assuage.

Jim went back into the kitchen and watched Charles, seemingly engrossed in an article, as he stood in the doorway. He tried to strain his eyes to see what he was reading, but Charles, noticing him, shut the magazine and was about to get up.

'Wait. Do you feel like a job?' He tried unsuccessfully to keep the edge out of his voice.

'What sort of a job?'

'A very nasty one. The roof of the animal's shelter needs patching.' A puddle was forming round him on the flags. 'I'll lend you some suitable gear.'

'My father was a DIY enthusiast,' Charles said cynically. 'Not that he achieved much. Myself I was never much for home improvements.'

'Well, this is not hanging pictures or putting up shelves.

Hard graft. Dirty unpleasant wet work.' Jim grinned. 'And –'
he laughed outright, 'now – a matter of livelihood. Nan's and
my livelihood. And yours, come to that.' Jim enjoyed these
lies.

'Give me the gear,' Charles said, getting up and putting the
magazine on the top of the dresser. Jim wondered if it was
porn.

Jim produced wellingtons and an old mac, thinking, This
won't suit your sartorial outlook, and they went out into the
rain.

They squelched through the gap that led into the cows'
field. A sheet of galvanised was embedded in weeds. 'Mind
you don't cut yourself.' They heaved it into place over the
struts of the lean-to and he instructed Charles to wait while he
foraged for bolts and a spanner. He was secretly brimming
with laughter. 'This'll make him take a U-turn home,' he
thought, rummaging round the outhouse, deliberately delay-
ing the next move. But when he returned Charles had cannily
manoeuvred himself into a dry niche and held the sheet in
place. Jim climbed in and began to adjust the nuts and bolts.

'Your tone of voice addressing Nan this morning was out of
order. Your sarcasm was palpably obvious. Nan is a famous
woman and I hope you have inherited even an iota of her
imagination.' He waited for the retort, but Charles continued
to hold the roof as though he hadn't heard.

When the job was finished, Charles calmly walked back
into the kitchen, kicked off the boots and retrieved his
magazine from the dresser.

So Charles plays his silent card, Jim thought. OK, so he too
would keep his cool. If this is the rude way he wants to carry
on, let him. He chose to forget his own rudeness earlier that
morning. In his chest there was a tightness, though, that he
knew could only be mitigated by both of them adopting a
less superior attitude. But what did he expect from this
arriviste, this parvenu, claiming a bloodline to his wife? Was

he supposed to make the first move, say please make yourself at home, dismantle our lives? *Mi casa e su casa.* The love business – mother love, child love, husband and wife love, love of place, animals, life – seemed to have deserted all three. He watched the kettle as it stopped boiling, automatically heating the coffee pot, bringing down three cups, spooning in the coffee, pouring the water in the way in which he and Nan used to celebrate life every day, and he wondered if those moments could somehow be retrieved if his voice kept pace with his common sense. Instead of sarcastic innuendos he must soften his tones, pummel the seeds of hatred into submission.

'I wonder, would you tell Nan coffee's made?'

Charles got up. 'Sure.'

Jim watched him leave the room, his stride manicured into carefulness. How totally unlike Nan, whose shoulders moved independently. His shoulders were stiffly taut, their expression wary. How awful to be him. He poured the coffee.

As a little girl, how Nan had loved just to look at the notes on the stave, like sparrows on a wire, and how simple it was learning their value. Crochets, quavers, demi-semi-quavers, minims, the symbol for the treble clef like an American dollar. Her father had sat her on his knee on her fourth birthday and told her about the piano that was coming. An old Collard and Collard he'd bought at an auction. And how, when he wasn't looking, she had climbed up and opened it and marvelled at the velvety feel of the hammers and the strings like a harp. But Lizzie was the one who must learn to play it first. Biddy O'Gorman, the village dressmaker, was employed to teach Lizzie the notes. But her lack of an ear was phenomenal and their father was stricken. Had he wasted his money and all the trouble they had gone to?

The three men puffing and heaving it up the steps and into

the parlour. When she asked if she could try she was told to wash the jam off her fingers and be sure not to touch the notes unless her grubby hands were clean. Also mother wasn't well and must not be disturbed. She said she would touch the keys as if they were also covered in velvet. Please, Miss O'Gorman, please. From then on Lizzie's torture was over. And also the torture for the rest of them! Her mother was better, too, and able to walk around again and cling to Lizzie, who was blonde and gentle, so they pressed their faces together and it didn't matter she had played off-key, sometimes doubling the notes as though to get the piece over more quickly. Her father was disappointed, a little stiff at first, with her, Nan, as though she had jumped further forward than he'd bargained for. As though he would have preferred for her to sit and watch, a little Miss Muffet on a cushion, not really part of the grown-up world. So sometimes he played himself, roughly. The Blue Danube, and Souza's marches. Or tunes from Gilbert and Sullivan. *The Mikado* or *The Pirates of Penzance*. How she loved to hear him sing:

> A wandering minstrel I,
> a thing of shreds and patches,
> of ballad songs and snatches
> and dreaming lullabies.

So was her career, begun on that old brocaded piano stool with its two cushions, suddenly over? Would her long life devoted to one end grind to a halt like an old car in a rutted boreen? Is this what happened when people got a stroke? Meaningless words tumbling out of their mouths? Or if she played, would she no longer be able to distinguish one sound from another?

When Charles came in, saying, 'Coffee's made,' she looked round at him . . .

'Thanks.'

'So this is where you hide? Like a crow on a perch, looking

down at those who can't fly.'

She searched for that other Nan. That cipher they wanted.

'That must have cost a pretty penny.' He came over and touched the piano.

'It's a hard graft,' she said, her voice nearly inaudible.

'Funny, that's what Jim said about mending the shed.' He turned and left the room.

She crouched on the piano stool. Dark and Kafkaesque.

PART IV

'WE USUALLY GET DRUNK ON CHRISTMAS EVE,' she heard Jim say as he shook himself into his gabardine overcoat. She had seen him earlier, spick and span, his balding hair smoothed over. 'So we are going to Rogan's to meet the Swanns,' he told Charles.

The previous ten days he had surprised Nan by remaining sober, going to bed early, immersing himself in his notes during the day. His meetings with Charles were conducted in a careful manner. Unable to grasp the reason for Jim's volte-face, she had wandered from room to room, opening and shutting the piano lid, annotating Jackson's piece, but unable to touch the keys. She removed the music from the top of the piano and buffed the surface till it reflected her face, then she'd sit and gaze at the four walls, hunched up in layers of woollen garments and from time to time blowing on her fingers. She didn't know what kept Charles busy. Most of the day he'd be found sitting by the range with the oven door open, a book held near his face. Once Jim had taken him out to show him where the hay was kept and how much meal he gave to the chickens.

Nan had watched them from the windows and overheard Charles saying, 'Are you thinking of leaving all this to me?' his collar turned up round his chin.

'I've been offered a job in Sydney. Nan is forgetful. Her work concentration is all-consuming.' His breezy lies danced in the thin air. She turned away in disgust.

Conversation between himself and her had ebbed to bare inanities: 'It's still raining,' 'It'll snow probably,' 'Will it?'

'That fucking door needs a new hinge,' 'Does it?'

She refused to go to Rogan's. They slept with their backs to each other. The house itself seemed to have become hostile – draughts, hitherto unimportant, whistled through cracks, damp wall patches threatened to spread – but strangely Charles seemed to ignore these shortcomings, closed away as he was in a coat of silence and cynicism.

They were clattering about in the hall. She sat absolutely still, trying to ward off her panic, the dread of her motherhood becoming public property. It was as if she were stepping off the mail boat that October morning thirty-one years ago, constantly looking over her shoulder, paranoid that her secret would be discovered. 'No, no, no,' she cried to the four walls. No. Nobody must know.

The previous night she had agreed that she would accompany them on Christmas Eve, but faced with it she was consumed with terror. They would talk. They would stare at her. She was not like Them. Once They knew, she could never relax again in the locality. She heard Jim shouting, but she sat on, huddled and lifeless.

'Nan,' his voice resounded in the hall. When she didn't answer he came into her room.

'I'm not coming.'

'But it's Christmas Eve.' Jim stood with his hand on the open door.

'Shut the fucking door,' she screamed.

'Charles is all dressed up, waiting for you.'

'Is he?'

'What about the Swanns? Nan, I can't go without you.' He shut the door and went over to her. He tried to put his arms around her but she wriggled away.

'I can't come,' she whispered. 'Please leave me alone.'

'But what are you afraid of? What is it?'

'You'll talk. The Swanns will talk.'

'God!' he said, trying to keep the irritability out of his tones. 'Nothing will be said. For heaven's sake, Nan.' He lifted her coat, which was on the chair, and brought it over to her.

'All right!' Her voice was shrill. 'On one condition. None must know Charles's parentage. I can't stand poking stares. Even the Swanns. I wish I'd never told them.'

When in the hall, she turned on Charles. 'And you. Don't say anything. Anything at all about me. I want it as if it were thirty years ago and the whole world ignorant of what I'd done.'

The two men, silenced by her outburst, about to pack into the car, were pushed aside.

'I'll drive,' she said, banging shut the door.

Nick was in the pub without Angela. She'd be down later. 'She's making the stuffing.'

Ignoring him, Nan went to the bar. She bought two pints and a large vodka.

'Are you not going to introduce us?' The doctor was giving no quarter. 'Oh, yes. Charles Fordson, Dr Swann. Nick.' She carried the pints to the shelf.

Charles looked round at the company as if he had never seen the like. Pat Mullen swaying on his heels, a group of Northerners screeching at each other as though they were in a high wind. Raphael Gilsenan was glowering into his pint and a knot of youngsters kept coming into the bar for cans of Coke and change for the pool table. And Nick, with a grin, began to engage Charles in conversation. 'How do you like it here?' But Charles, who had just had his pint jostled, cried, 'Mind out,' and Nan was mortified by his accent, which didn't seem so noticeable at home.

The evening opened into pre-Christmas mayhem. A Country and Western two-piece band carried in enough amps for an orchestra and began to tune up. And after Nick, wolfish, had probed into Charles's reactions to rural Ireland and the latter had downed his second pint, he began to talk.

'My mother used to make a big thing about Christmas. She'd spend days and days shopping, bringing in parcels wrapped in coloured paper and hiding them under the tree. Very traditional, she was. Father was kept at bay. She would have tied him down if she could, but on Christmas Day there was always a crisis. Something would have been forgotten. Tin foil. Cranberry sauce, crackers. They'd rant at each other, she more angry, he more sullen. And I'd play with my toys in the corner, my helicopters, racing cars, gadgets that lit up and broke, till everything lay in a muddle of wrapping paper and cardboard boxes and I bawled my head off... That was when I was small, of course. After, it was different.'

As he talked, people shoved against them while they balanced their drinks, lit cigarettes with one hand, and they all stared at him. Finally Angela came in and suggested they should dance. The band played 'Galway Bay' three four three four and the Swanns took to the floor.

'We'd better have a go,' Jim said to Nan, watching her carefully. 'Vodkas, do the job!' he prayed silently.

But she, who loved dancing, wouldn't dance. 'Charles,' she said, 'did you not have one good Christmas?'

'Oh, fuck Christmas,' Jim said, and pulled her out on the floor.

But after a few steps, she said, 'No, Jim. He'll blab,' and went back to Charles. '*You* talk when you're drunk,' she spat at him.

The group reunited. Nick asked Jim what he was cooking tomorrow. 'Nothing.' Nick shifted. Women in high-heeled shoes and flouncy dresses, men in sleeveless jumpers and

open-necked shirt, swirled round. Fiona and Matt ran from
end to end of the bar, pulling pints and half-ones. Jim ordered
another round, but Charles said he'd had enough. 'But you've
only had a few pints.' 'Isn't that enough?' Nick, more wolfish
than ever, and Angela asked them were they coming to pre-
prandial drinks tomorrow, and Jim said they had a table
booked at Grants. 'Haven't we?' He turned to Nan.

'I didn't book it.'

'In that case,' Angela said, wondering at such incompetency
at Christmas of all times, 'you'd better join us. We'll eat about
four.'

In the jacks, Angela and Nan coincided, the former commenting on Charles's good looks. 'Interesting what he was
saying, wasn't it?'

'Drink talks.'

'How's Jim?'

'Sober.'

Nan threw paper over the partition. They peed in unison.

'What the hell's got into you?' Angela wanted to say, but
left it.

Back with the three men, Nan searched their faces. What
had they been saying? She had drunk too quickly and she tried
to steady herself. She must get Charles away somehow. Take
him into a corner. Tell him to shut up. In crazy desperation,
she turned on him. 'Perhaps you'd like to dance?' And half
stumbling, half running, she pulled him out on the floor.

The three of them stared after the couple. 'What do you
know?' Nick said, meeting Angela's eyes, while the latter, out
of the corner of her mouth, said, 'How sweet!'

Jim turned his back on her, insensitive cow.

It was a fast number and the couples were whirling and
cavorting, Nan and Charles also. Jim was surprised to see
how good a dancer he was. He kept pace with the rhythm
while controlling Nan, who looked on the point of falling.

'Not that bad, old man.' Nick gave Jim a purifying glance.

'Isn't Nan more relaxed?'

'I don't know how Nan is. We haven't met since this creature arrived.'

'Post-Charles stress syndrome,' said Angela, and the two of them went out on the floor again.

Jim ordered a secret whiskey. Another short would do the trick. And then he'd tell them the unvarnished truth. Which was? What was the unvarnished truth? He knocked back the drink and ordered another.

But Nan now knew only her terror that Charles, who had gone to the toilet, would blurt out his lineage to all and sundry out of spite. Bitter bastard. What was she to do? She was so drunk she couldn't even talk straight. Was he really vicious or was it just his aloneness? He thinks he's among enemies, so he may use any weapons that come to hand. Misery superimposed her terror. 'Nobody knows how hard I've worked,' she shouted at them. 'All down the years. No one knows what it's like to keep going with all the competition. Every day I'm more and more terrified I'll be kicked aside. Thrown out like an old boot. And Jim there sits on his arse and does fuck all, and now, when I'm in this God-awful predicament with Charles, he attacks me. I wish I'd told him about all this before we married, then we wouldn't be married. You'd have married that Fiona McCarthy one and be separated long ago. What a balls-up.' And she flounced out of the pub.

Simultaneously the others stood up for the National Anthem. No sign of Charles. Jim wondered if he was being sick.

The two Swanns said good night and that they'd pick up Nan if they saw her. Jim was left on his own with the dregs of a pint.

Christmas Eve!

When Jim got up, there was no sign of either Charles or Nan.

Perhaps the former had killed himself and the latter was at the Swanns'. He felt cheerful with no hangover. Christmas morning and not a sinner to be seen. He threw some detergent into a basin and began to scrub the table.

He had noticed a thin skin of ice when he'd driven home and he looked out to check what further damage had been created while he slept. The grass was stiff with a coating of frost and the spruce had been dusted as well. A white Christmas. Soon Bing Crosby's voice would ring out on the radio and everyone would be happy and there'd be lots of people killed on the roads as families skidded to each other's houses, all the tinsel and coloured paper parcels scattered on the ice.

He and Nan never spread themselves at Christmas, simply bought each other a present. His gift for Nan he had purchased in Dublin and carefully hidden all these months. But what would she have for him? Would she have anything at all? He felt the familiar cloud darkening his mind. Could they ever pick up the bits again? Find that ease between them that they used to slip into? Like slipping your foot into a comfortable shoe.

He picked up the phone.

The eldest of the Cygnets answered and said Mummy and Daddy were still in bed and she didn't know whether Nan had stayed or not. Would she check, please? His hand shook as he reached for the kettle, cradling the receiver under his ear. 'Dear God, let Nan be safe. And not lying in a ditch dead from hypothermia. I'm a cynical bastard, but I'd die if anything happened to her. Even if she doesn't know or has forgotten who I am. Please.' 'Are you there?' 'Yes.' 'Nan's in the spare room.' The receiver rocked on its cradle as he replaced it. 'The fucking bitch.' Jim had now coated himself so well in this veneer of cynical tolerance he found himself again believing that he really didn't care one way or the other how things panned out. He was tired. Physically tired from all the distorted emotions. He felt he could only let things lie till some balance was achieved without his interference.

And Charles appeared, neatly dressed as ever. 'Your mother – how ridiculous – is at the Swanns'. The couple we were with last night.'

'I know who the Swanns are. They seem pleasant types.'

'Pleasant? Nick and Angela are cunning hoors. But pleasant?'

'Is there anything to eat in this place?'

'Did we have supper last night? I forget.'

Charles said he ought to take a stand. He rummaged around for bread.

'Mother's a disgrace.'

'Don't call her that.'

'You just did.'

'Nan is Nan. And she's not a disgrace.' He felt grumpy now and didn't care for this badinage.

So his fears for Nan's safety had been groundless. He felt a fool. Praying! Nan is too clever to die. But . . .

'The weather is of grave interest. Driving, drunk or sober, is inadvisable. So in an hour or so we'll walk to the Swanns'. For annual Christmas drinks.' He slunk into his study.

Nan had no idea where she was. The wall was on the wrong side of the bed. A cold hot-water bottle lay near her toes. She curled up her legs to absorb a little body warmth. She searched her mind for continuity. She had heard someone come into her room a while ago when she was half awake. Could she be in Poland? Could that have been the hotel maid wanting to clear her out while she made the bed? Gradually, through the opening and shutting of her brain, things began to clarify. She had flounced out of Rogan's. And she was at the Swanns'. How embarrassing. But how did she get here? She had no recollection of the journey. She raised herself up and pulled back a chink of curtain. Frost. She burrowed back under the bedclothes. And Charles. Dear God, Charles. They had danced. She had become drunk and stupid. Had she made things worse by her outburst?

She was trundling back down that road. That road pitted with potholes. Elsie was crying. Crying for her, Nan's lack of heart. That was it. Heart. Why didn't she have a heart? Why wasn't she like other women? No wonder Jim was fed up with her. God, she prayed, let Jim have got home safe. Let him not have skidded into a ditch. If he has, it will be her fault. Even if he doesn't give a shit about me, please don't let harm have come on him. This cold morning it no longer seemed to matter what Charles said or did. She simply wanted to get to Jim, find him somehow, behind all the screens he had erected between them. She leapt out of bed, shuffling into her garments, and ran downstairs.

Angela was in the kitchen, beslippered, in a woollen dress-ing gown. Her long hair was tied up on the top of her head and screwed into a knot. She looked fresh and washed. 'Happy Christmas.'

'That as well. And ice.' She asked the time and was told it was half eleven. 'Was I terrible last night?'

'You were a bit upset. We were worried.'

Nan combed her fingers through the knots in her hair. 'I'm sorry. I am really. I'll try to sort things better. I'll try.' She felt near tears. 'Talk to them. Both together, do you think?'

Angela sucked in her cheeks. 'For your sake, anyway.'

'You mean to hell with the men?' She had wanted to say, Fuck them, but the morning was too clean, too Christmassy.

'Something like that,' Angela said.

She wished she could be of use. To stand with a dish towel in her hand as she did when visiting her brother's wife. She wanted to be normal. Not someone who travelled the world and had given a baby away without a qualm. Angela wouldn't have done that. And Nick would have made a decent woman of her by marrying her. She was older than Angela. Nearly ten years older. And that meant the world had been that much more unforgiving by half a generation when she was young.

'Can I please wash the dishes?'

Angela was torn between Christmas hospitality and the desire to get rid of her to get on with the work. 'Perhaps I should run you home, so as you can all be back here around three o'clock. The girls are good on Christmas Day. The season's generosity rubs off on them.'

Nan was mortified. 'Oh, Angela, I'll walk.'

The frosty air scorched her face. The road was a sheet of ice. Virginal. There was absolute quiet. With each step she skidded and nearly lost momentum. A young lad on a tractor approached and she had to slide into the hedge. The machine danced from side to side with no control, its burden of silage bales on the trailer wagging uncertainly. Cattle must be fed. More important than humans. What is wrong with us? Why can't we three be friends? This has happened to hundreds of people lately. Children finding long-lost parents and vice versa. And you hear it brings nothing but happiness. It's all my fault. I must mend it. I must. With dry mouth and thumping head, she slithered on.

In the kitchen she stood by the range to thaw out. She noticed the scrubbed table and felt useless. Christmas morning, when every woman in Ireland, except she, was preparing, cutting, selecting, secure in the knowledge of their being needed, prized and loved.

The demolished turkey lay on its dish like a rusting car. They all had paper hats on and the two girls were reading the stale jokes that came with the crackers.

Nick, *pater familias*, had been boisterous, which he seldom was, and he got up to fetch the brandy. Jim had made coffee, which none drank, and Patricia, the eldest said, 'Now Nan, give us a tune!'

Nan was bloated with food and drink, and she was half conscious that Charles had made an effort to chat up Shona. Was that good or bad? She no longer knew. The lowest and highest notes were mute, but the rest of the instrument was just playable. Both the Cygnets had been taught to read music but neither of them was interested. Only happy when astride a horse. Nan wondered what would have happened to her if her father had never bought that Collard and Collard. Would she have taught herself a guitar and become a guitar bore like half the younger population of Ireland? A beautiful instrument but only played well by about one in a thousand. She sat down at the keyboard and said 'Requests?'

'A Beatles number,' the girls shouted in unison, knowing that Nan came from the generation of Beatlemania, so she started up with 'Love Me Do', battering the ancient piano into submission.

Then it was Angela's turn to sing and she began with 'Carrickfergus'. Nick sang along with her till Jim joined in.

'Now Charles,' Angela said. 'Give us a song.'

'I don't sing.'

'Everyone sings.'

'Christmas Day at home was a quiet day, once Mother had calmed down.'

'But the English always break into song. What about all those great cockney songs? Music-hall numbers? She was poor but she was honest, victim of a rich man's purse, et cetera?'

Charles's face darkened. Nan rejoined them and sat down beside him. 'Charles, you're among friends. You don't have to sing.' Even the girls quietened down. Everyone gazed at them. She put her hand over his, felt the stiffened muscle of his arms, the small hairs standing up at the curl of his wrists. She ran her hand further up his sleeve. Then she lifted his hand and put the back of it against her cheek.

Silence. Embarrassment. Patricia pulled the last cracker with

Shona. Nan looked at each one in turn, at the lowered eyes, the tidying of cutlery. Nick quickly poured more brandy and said, 'A toast to the cook.'

Charles, as silent as the others, raised his glass, having pulled away from Nan, who also raised hers and waved it in Angela's direction. They all agreed the dinner had been a culinary miracle.

Jim said, 'On this day of all days', and the literate laughed. He felt he had behaved impeccably during the entire day. He had helped to carry in the laden platters, fetched the holly for the Christmas pudding, removed the dinner plates at exactly the right moment and never once sneered at Charles. In fact, he had been shocked by Angela's clumsiness.

Before dinner they had attempted a Christmas walk. The roads were impossible, so they had gone across the fields, skirting into Gilsenan's territory. Jim was worried, because it was the first Christmas they hadn't brought Pat Mullen his turkey dinner. He didn't dare ask Angela if she'd give him a plate for him. So he guiltily crept past his house. The walk had petered out quite soon and they'd returned to more drinks in the drawing room, while Angela and the girls put the finishing touches to the meal. Nick, old-fashioned as the breadwinner, 'left it to the women', so Nan, Nick, Jim and Charles wandered around, setting up ashtrays, picking up wrapping paper and drinking sherry.

'For the dinner we are reserving an exclusive hock,' Nick clinically stated, and Nan felt guilty for only having brought two bottles of ordinary wine and a bottle of sloe gin.

Christmas night. Jim, Angela and the two girls were in the kitchen, so this time it was Charles, Nan and Nick who wandered round in post-prandial fog. Angela was a cunning governor of the house, she knew exactly how to enter Christmas Day and tunnel right through it without mishap. Although it seemed she had drunk just as much as everyone else, she had stayed brown and wholesome throughout. She wore earrings that chimed as she bent her head and her tan-coloured tussore suit was quietly alluring.

Nan felt ill-clad in a pale green woollen dress, although she wore a beautiful gold necklace with a filigree pendant that Jim had bought her in Budapest. But Jim thought secretly she was the most striking of the two. The Cygnets, in their miniskirts, however, thought Nan a frump compared with their mother. What Charles thought, no one knew.

On St Stephen's Day they walked again. For miles. This time without the Swanns. The ice had melted. A route march across fields and roads, skirting the lake, climbing barbed-wire fences with sheep hair clinging to them. They walked in silence, Charles striding out in front, like a young English squire in his waisted gabardine. A fairy mist coated the land and puffed around a fox's covert which the hunt had recently left, causing hoof marks of mud in the gaps between the fields. Nan got repeated shafts of embarrassment, remembering her behaviour the previous night. She had been out of order. Rebuffed, humiliated. But then, she had admitted her panic. Why not? It was Angela's insensitivity that had caused her misjudged action. OK. They had 'got over' Christmas, that primitive hurdle of the winter solstice, and after this the days would lengthen and their windows grow a fraction brighter every morning.

And . . .

Perhaps . . .

Perhaps she and Jim and Charles would finally talk to each other. But, like food that's lain in the fridge too long, would the germs of poison still be lurking?

At the top of the brae they could hear the hounds in the distance. The riders, half dead from hangovers, could barely cling to their mounts. They waited to catch sight of the field, expecting to see the two Cygnets in the van. Sure enough

Patricia on her chestnut was well in front, but no sign of Shona. Maybe she had fallen and gone home in a pet. Nan remembered her own efforts to catch up with her sister and how every year the goalposts were altered. God help the youngest of the family.

She was just then struck by the fact that Jim and Charles were only sons. Was that significant? No sibling rivalry during childhood. Should she point this out to Swann? she wondered. The nub of the problem? But not simple at all.

There were three standing stones in the next field behind a ruined cottage and this was usually the end of their trip. A yearly pilgrimage into the past. Would Jim tell Charles what they were?

When they came first, Jim had covered his sketchbook with drawings of unexpected dolmens or passage graves, comparing his findings with those of the existing inch maps and being delighted if any of them had been ignored, but by now he had pretty well exhausted the adjacent countryside.

If they travelled on now they would reach Lough Macnean, lake of the bird's son, but they were tired, soaked from the fine mist. They turned for home.

Charles had displayed little interest in the terrain but had soldiered on without complaint. The hunt had disappeared and Nan hoped they hadn't killed the fox. Sly as a fox, cute as a fox, drunk as an owl, sick as a dog. What rubbish we humans indulge in. If it were the other way around, we'd be thought a joke!

Thus her thoughts rambled, hopeful one minute, scared the next. She threw wistful looks at Jim from time to time. His painfully cheerful mood over the last two days had left her washed out and confused. As they finally came in sight of home, she began to wonder if Jim cared at all. Was he even glad? Was he using Charles as an excuse to get rid of her?

Would he leave her now? Gather up his notes, his goods, his affection, and walk away into the horizon of their relationship? Yet she knew it was Charles she should curse. But she couldn't curse him. The atmosphere was fast becoming untenable. Sooner or later something had to break.

All three in their varied states of hostility entered the house.

Jim had banked up the stove and the kitchen opened its arms to them. He remembered his grandfather, after he'd retired, who always welcomed him on his return from Blackrock College. How he sat at the range, tapping his pipe, and he'd say, 'Ah, Jim,' and the dottle would hiss on the red-hot plate. A whole world of security. The old man had outlived Jim's mother by fifteen years, and he remembered his grandfather's eyes as her coffin was lowered, his sorrow having no name. He could not reach words that day, nor for many days afterwards. But he eventually shadowed his grief by his love for his grandson. The old man had loved books and he introduced Jim to all the old favourites, Rider Haggard, Alexandre Dumas, exciting stories of long-gone heroes, of the Greek and Egyptian gods, the Celtic legends and myths. It was to him he owed his curiosity for the distant past. How was it that his father had faded from his memory and only his mother and grandfather were the beacons of his past? His father, the civil servant who had taken the Shankhill bus punctually every morning at a quarter to eight and who came home every night quietly exhausted and turned on the wireless to listen to the nine o'clock news, who didn't take a drink and went to bed at ten. He was a small rotund man, unlike his grandfather, who had a rangy old frame, and he clipped his grey moustache with nail scissors and ate his morning porridge standing up, adding a little salt to it. His going to work left no trace. It was as though he didn't go through doors. When finally Jim was going to college they took the same bus into Dublin. Neither spoke.

When the bus was crowded they occupied separate seats and Jim was relieved when this happened, although their mutual silence never bothered him.

But that was all so long ago and now it was St Stephen's Day in the 1990s and this taciturn Englishman was sharing their board, a stranger. A stranger with the ties of blood to his wife. Long ago he would have been exploring the Wicklow hills on this day, dodging the Anglo-Irish estates, those ana-chronistic bastions of the past. Their children would have been following the Bray Harriers. Instead of now, when the hunt was owned by a German industrialist who had bought a mansion and enclosed himself in signs of 'Trespassers will be prosecuted' and 'Private property'. Anyone less eccentric or less Anglo-Irish it would be hard to imagine.

A frothing Rottweiller stood guard at the gate lodge, which was let out each summer for fabulous weekly sums. Bunches of young bankers or civil servants would rent it at weekends, wearing open-toed sandals and loose clothing in the freezing spring weather, or other Germans would come in their four-wheel drives or Dormobiles, with bicycles strapped on the back and Deutschmarks in their bum-belts. Was all this a change for the better or the worse? Who knows?

Perhaps it was better if an Irish couple turned one of those mansions into an exclusive hotel, like Grants, where they had intended to eat yesterday, couples who had studied in Switzerland and worked their way up through the barbed wire of ambition and finally achieved their goal. What then? They had no further to go. They had refurbished the elegant Georgian rooms, installed central heating, bathrooms en-suite, combed the sweep of the avenue, dusted the herbaceous borders and waited for the Americans to be unloaded from their buses, elderly and exhausted. At night maybe a discreet harpist, a colleen with golden locks, would play settings of Yeats poems while they dreamed of their condominiums in California. Had they not all come from the auld sod, a thatched cottage with the pig in the parlour, and wasn't it a bit of luck that they still weren't there? Jim also allowed his thoughts to ramble on, needing to ignore both Nan and Charles, who had plunged themselves in newspapers to avoid speaking, he supposed.

He looked at his wife, bundled up in a green (green suited her) Aran sweater, her hair spiked in a comb on the top of her head. A Goya, indeed at rest, and his heart filled. How could he consider for a moment living without her? He wished, how he wished, that Charles, whom he might even get to like, would go away. Vanish overnight like the frost. And then. Then what? Pretend he had never been. Never lived.

When Jim went into his study, Charles dropped his paper. He looked over at his mother. His mother Nanny Wine. His real mother, of course, was Victoria Fordson. Nan was a substitute. An image of the real thing. Victoria had been stupid but well meaning and Nan was the opposite of both.

'You never wanted to meet me, did you?'

'I . . .'

'No. I know.'

She laid down her paper. 'For the last thirty years I have thought about you nearly every day.'

'Not me, you haven't. But an ephemeral being. A ghost of the past.'

'No. I watched you in my mind at various stages of your life, especially your early childhood. As an adult I wasn't too sure.

'You have played at storytelling.'

She got up to make more coffee and to shut the study door.

'And what do you mean by my not wanting to meet you? I made a choice, didn't I? I could have refused. For the sake of Jim's and my relationship. And it's you. It's you who have been relentlessly unfriendly since we met.'

'Wait.'

'No, you told your story that first night in the restaurant.

Why? To make me guilty. Since then you've kept your distance. What am I supposed to do? Is there room for bargaining or has too much damage been done? Last night I behaved sloppily and, if I offended your sensibilities, I'm sorry. I was drunk. I know I can't make up for thirty years of neglect by stroking your hand. Indeed, I'm embarrassed when I think of it.'

'I'm not thinking of that. Of course, I was pretty disgusted.'

'Don't use words like that,' Nan shouted. 'That's typical of you. The way you slide in cutting remarks.' Now she was going down the road she wanted to avoid. 'What do you want? Do you want to blame me for your parents' ignorance?'

'They weren't ignorant. They were confused. They did what they thought was the right thing. Let's face it, you and Jim can't wait to get rid of me, just as you couldn't wait to get rid of your baby.'

She wanted to explain that had she kept him, it might have been worse living in sleazy furnished rooms, being thrown out for lack of money for the rent, going from pillar to post. But words could not be assembled. There were too many sides to the coin. She wanted to tell him how she'd worked in a factory for six months. How she'd vomited behind the machine, worn corsets to hide her pregnancy and finally, when she was too huge, she'd gone to that filthy hostel to be bullied and insulted by an insane woman. And then. At last. She was what? Free. Free to come home. Free to study. Free to use something that she alone had. Her unique talent.

But he knew. Of course he knew all that, and now, for the same reason, in her late forties, her career might end. She was boxed in on all sides. And the only thing she could find to say was, 'I was fifteen . . . a kid. She called me Oirish.'

He started to laugh. 'Think I don't know. What you and Jim think . . . Never in your wildest dreams would either of you admit to having an English relation.'

'But you are not English.'

'That's where you're wrong. What do I know about the Irish? I have no family here. Just an uncomfortable couple called Nan and Jim McDonald. I'll leave tomorrow.'

'No!' Her voice rose. 'No! I'm finished either way. My career is over.'

Charles started to get up, his lips so thin they'd nearly disappeared. 'Don't be dramatic.'

'Wait.' She was spinning out of control. 'Please. Let's try . . .'

'Try what? To make me Irish? To throw off all my English inhibitions and take on some phoney persona that would have no value for any of the three of us? No. If you want bargaining, then you must accept my English upbringing – whose fault was that? – and then we might make a move in the right direction.'

'I personally have nothing against the English. Possibly my best friend ever was English. Elsie, a girl I met in the hostel. She was older than me. I learned a lot from her. But I'm only asking you to accept that we are Irish. By upbringing, mores, however good or bad, relations, political outlook. Can you accept that?'

Charles got up and went to the window. He drew the curtains. His shoulders were full of anger. When he turned round his skin had darkened. He rushed over and banged the table with his fist. 'You'll never understand.' The cutlery jumped and Nan, paralysed, wanted to cry out for Jim, but her mouth was parched. Nothing belonged to her any more.

He leant over the table and hissed into her face. 'There were relations of my father's. A brother, Uncle Jasper. He gave me a train set on my sixteenth birthday. You see, once they had told me I wasn't their child, they didn't know where to turn. They tried to make up to me in all sorts of different ways. But when I didn't react gratefully to my uncle's ridiculous gesture, my father flew into a rage and told me I was an ungrateful whelp. The word made me think of a puppy, something to be slapped and put out and told not to pee on the carpet. I had just been let out of hospital. They were afraid of me. Mother, especially. When father acted like that she shrank. Her face became grey. It was pitiful.'

'Please, Charles. It's over.'

She had felt his spit on her face and she, too, shrank back. But suddenly his violence left him. He fell heavily into the opposite chair, his shoulders loosened, his chin dropped to his chest. He lay back and closed his eyes.

That was how Jim found them a few moments later. Two figures frozen, one on each side of the table. A painting by a German expressionist of the 1940s or 1950s? Otto Dix, perhaps. He went to the dresser and brought down three glasses and poured them each a measure of whiskey.

Jim looked at his wife. Heavy, listless. Numbed, he watched her drag herself from the room.

Who was this man who had insinuated his – what, madness? – into their lives? He bent to pick up the chair she had knocked over. Sitting himself in it, he spoke slowly, like a police interrogator.

'Did he beat you?'

'Good lord, no.' Charles didn't open his eyes.

'Her?'

'Not her either.' He yawned. 'He wouldn't have had the know-how.'

'What do you want to do, Charles?'

'I don't know. I simply don't know. I've messed everything up. I know Nan was only trying to be friendly last night when she made that awkward gesture. And I shouldn't have reacted like I did. I felt murderous just now. I could have killed her.'

Jim saw Charles's past stripped in front of him. The long grey years. Parents 'doing the right thing' for this impostor. This alien. And he saw Charles like a piece of sculpture with a hole in its belly. And he felt something extraordinary creeping over him. Something he didn't understand then, but much later described to himself as a paternal glow. This man sixteen or so years younger than he could have been his son.

He let a silence settle between them. Charles had arrived in shock. A bare few months after his parents had died. Been viciously killed, in fact. And he expected to find what? Something he had never known, so he couldn't put a name to it.

And all he'd found was a self-satisfied couple in a foreign country . . .

The darkness of St Stephen's Day crept around them. The man opposite didn't stir, his fair head resting on his chest, and Jim saw something that shocked him. Two tears trickling down his cheekbones. Two tiny smears that fell into nowhere after glistening on the edge of his chin.

It was now quite black outside. He riddled the range. The pale gold of the untouched whiskey reflected the light. His head was full of unspoken clichés: It's not Nan's fault. She did what she thought best. Can we sort this out sensibly? Do you want to stay or go back to that empty village? But he walked the tightrope of indecision. He must wait for the other to make the first overture of friendship which might avert some appalling tragedy.

He didn't believe in the other's angry mouthings but he was frightened for Nan. She might lose her step and enter that black tunnel at the end of which there would be no light. He had a sudden memory of the river in which he used to swim as a child. And how it tunnelled under the aqueduct and water dripped from the arched stones like wine into a glass. And how he had often stood, daring himself to dive in. But the dark waters scared him, had a foetid smell, as if the souls of drowned people lurked there. Was it like this with Nan now? He tiptoed into her room. She had her back to him as she stared out at the night.

'Nan,' he whispered.

She swirled round at him and he saw something which stayed with him for a long time afterwards. A vision of what he could only describe as insubstantiality. As though her spirit had left her. That vibrant spirit that was hers alone.

PART V

WINTER TOOK ITS TOLL OF DEATHS. The most surprising of all was that of Maggie Slater, whom everyone thought would live for ever. Fonsie had rushed over. 'Mother's taken bad. I've rung the ambulance.' And Jim had fled through fields to find her in bed, where Fonsie had lain her, an old twig, her eyes, those small blue Slater eyes, filled with terror. 'You'll be all right,' Jim murmured, while Fonsie held her hand and the awful love this dry man had for his mother filled the room.

They could hear the sirens then and simultaneously Onion-head appeared at the door with the two ambulancemen. With Maggie on a stretcher, the two brothers followed her into the ambulance. She had died that night.

Then Matt Rogan's mother got pneumonia and for three days the pub was shut. Lawlor's got all the custom, so reluct-antly Matt opened up again, saying she was pulling through. A lie of course. She, too, died the following week.

As usual they attended the funerals, the biting winds sweep-ing through the graveyard. And the pubs stayed open all day. That is to say Jim did, Nan refusing to be seen in public.

In January Nan dragged herself to Limerick to play Jackson's piece. She still wasn't ready for it. After that awful row with Charles she had crept around the house avoiding him. She tried hard to concentrate on her work, but every so often her confidence ebbed away. A difficult piece, jumping from thirds to fifths after a long passage of staccato arpeggios, and if it hadn't been for Declan she would have cancelled the concert. But she couldn't let him down. And as she had foreseen, the result was a disaster. Declan did his best to reassure her, but she knew she had played so badly it was as if he were accompanying her instead of the other way round.

'I'm finished,' she screamed at Jim one night, as she threw herself on the bed.

He didn't know where to turn. He had never seen her like this. 'Will I tell Charles to leave?' he asked lamely.

'No no no! It makes no difference.' She clutched handfuls of the bedclothes, kicking out her legs like an epileptic. He tried to comfort her but she lunged out at him, screaming, 'Fuck you, fuck you!'

From time to time she did make an effort to practise, but after a few chords her interest would flag and she'd stay by the piano, listless, staring into space. A composer friend sent her a short piece for her to edit, but somehow the notes jingled in her head, a mish-mash of sound. She sent it back untouched. Eventually the house fell silent.

As time went on she made her bed in a tiny room beyond the bathroom, a room they used for household detritus – cardboard boxes, worn-out clothing, old shoes, holy pictures smudged and dampened with age. Here she hid from the two men, vaguely aware of the fact that they had become friends. As the days lengthened, it seemed to her that they were travelling through the winter world in another dimension. Nothing to do with her.

And in a strange way it was true. In their bewildered state the two men had turned to each other like conspirators, talking in whispers, as though the house were haunted. When they bumped into each other they'd go into Jim's study, where they felt safe, and Charles would tell how he had several times tried to talk to Nan, how he had sought her out to offer words of atonement, but she just looked at him as though he were invisible. And Jim would reiterate the same thing – how his overtures to Nan had been rebuffed. And Charles had tried to explain how much he wanted to say to her, 'I am your son, I was born in a dingy hostel in Cheapside, London, but now that Jim and I have smoothed out some of our differences, should the war not be over?' He asked Jim if it was all his fault, that terrible row on St Stephen's Day. But these tellings only added to Jim's malaise. When he tried to explain that he and Nan had lived so openly down the years he had no equipment to deal with her like this, and that he was deeply hurt by her leaving his bed, Charles listened in silence, till at length he simply said one day, 'I'll leave. It's the only solution.'

But this idea terrified Jim. In a sense he imagined that Charles back in England would be even more of a threat to his and Nan's ever sorting out their differences, and he suggested that maybe Nan only needed time to readjust. That instead of slinking around the house like thieves they should assert themselves by doing some work, carry on as if the world hadn't ground to a halt.

Secretly he could not allow himself to think that Nan was really ill, troubled by something beyond his comprehension. He just wanted the old Nan back. She must be there, he told himself, and any day now the three of them would sit around the table and talk.

So, in desperation, he tried to stir up some of his old enthusiasms. He went to Knowth, remembering his excitement when the tomb was finally opened, and how he had been part of that school outing in 1962 and the thrills of finding that our ancestors, who far from being what Mr Knowles deemed obstinately wild and wilfully improvident, were an imaginative, intelligent and inventive crew. Now he made sketches of the artistic kerbstones. He persuaded the very lovely young woman, a student of Cork, to give him carte blanche to wander at will outside the regular hours given to the public and lost himself in wonder once again. And the ever present question of why had Charles stayed, or, indeed, why he needed Charles to lean on, ceased to bother him. Each day he opened to him more. Especially when the other hinted that the sudden death of his parents, in spite of his mixed feelings, had shattered him. How his own shabby house in Crowsfort had filled him with disgust. That he had grown to like the Irish way of thinking, which at first he'd despised. So, grabbing at the threads of his earlier ambitions, he brought Charles into his space, his need to protect Charles an alternative to his need to protect Nan.

At home he spent time in his study, filing and putting notes together, and he persuaded Charles to join him on these excursions. Jim outlined what is known about the megalithic peoples of Ireland and Charles agreed to accompany him to the Bend of the Boyne. In Knowth he pointed out the intricate designs on the orthostats and the sandstone 'Baetyl' block. Showing how these are not just scratchings or doodles but how the stones had been carefully prepared, the surface having had a portion removed, which took time and skill, premising the possibility of their having some religious importance. He taught him to recognise a possible cyst as they drove through the countryside, and they would stop and count the ridges, laughing, as it is said that the more ridges the bigger the chief that is buried there! Together they began to study astro-archaeology and the importance these people must have attached to the equinoces, the quarter-years and the solstices. He took him to Audleystown in County Down to see the court tomb, to Armagh to see the Portal Tomb at Ballykeel, and to Carrowkeel in County Sligo. Here they climbed up on a blustery day, the panorama of Sligo and Roscommon laid out behind them, an undulating carpet.

They stood for ages as the clouds scythed the stones, the

heather and the lake, and for a second their eyes met, as though some strange mystery had been revealed to them.

So the winter had gone, Nan knew not where. She had wandered the silent house. Those nine months before Charles – Séan – was born echoed in her mind. As the men came and went on their travels, and she sat in her studio looking out at the night, at the moon sliding over the puddles, at the square of light on the grass cast by the kitchen window, she seemed anchored to that distant past. Sometimes she'd creep out of her room and roam the house, a troubled spirit, saying to herself, 'I must be lodged, I must be lodged.' She kept reliving that day when she had taken the mail boat, when her life was lying in shards around her. Then sometimes her mind would clear and she would wonder what she was doing. I must practise, she'd say, and she'd jump up and go to the piano. But once there her panic would overcome her and she'd rush upstairs and hide in her room.

She had been like this for months, it seemed. Until one evening she wandered right out of the house and, looking in at the kitchen, saw the two men, one each side of the table. There was a mess of half-open tins of beans, slices of ham, half-cut tomatoes, and she watched Jim get up and pile the food on Charles's plate. Both laughing. She couldn't hear what they were saying, but a bolt of anger shot through her. How dare they? How dare they destroy her spirit? She was filled with thoughts of revenge. As if they were waging gender warfare. 'Let them,' she screamed out loud. 'Just let them.' What did they want, anyway? For her to be a wife? A mother? 'I'll show you then,' she screamed again. 'And see how you like it.'

Because the Nan he loved no longer seemed to be there, Jim scarcely bothered to clear up after meals, leaving Charles to bundle things away as Jim shook himself into his study. He often said to Charles things like, 'I used to have a marriage' or 'I loved making the place spick for her.' And on these occasions Charles had to bring him round to the hope that she'd soon see sense, but in actual fact he believed that Nan was genuinely ill and that nothing would change until they got outside help. Therefore they both went into deep shock when she marched in that night. Quite calm, quite cool, saying, 'When you've finished your tea, you can clear up and fuck off to your various haunts. From now on I'll be here when you come home. Oh, yes. In this very kitchen.' Slowly each of them got up and left the room. They were unable to answer her. Her speech had clogged their tongues.

At first they were embarrassed by this. But then they looked on it as a good sign that she was interesting herself in anything at all. When they came home at night, red-cheeked from their excursions, she'd be there making their tea, with soup and sandwiches, and when they were cosily ensconced she'd disappear.

One day, as Charles was emptying the water out of their boots and stuffing newspaper into them, he shouted, 'We must do something. She hasn't eaten for weeks. She just shuts herself in that fucking piano room. I'm going to get the doctor. There must be someone in this god-damn country who can talk to her.'

'No, you're not,' Jim said coldly. 'I know my wife. Swann has lost interest anyway.'

'I'm not talking about Swann. A proper head-man.'

'She can't stand psychiatrists. She'll come round in time.'

'In time! In time. Always in time. How much time does she need? She's been like this for months. It's agreeable, isn't it, to have our dinner on the table when we come home from our games? Yes, games. We've been playing games, haven't we?'

Jim looked into Charles's piercing eyes, looked for his shame to be mirrored in them, but saw only defiance in the stance of a man holding a boot in his hand. A man waiting for him to come up with some solution.

He had tried to plunge himself into his work to avoid his mind's bankruptcy and Charles had called it 'games'. He said finally, 'Nan has shut herself behind her beauty and mystery. It's not only me who is to blame. But she is not mad. She knows what she is doing and she is punishing us. Let's give her a few more weeks. Please.'

Charles put the two boots upside down on the range, hung up his wet coat and sat down to his tea.

In April, warm for the time of year, Nan couldn't stand the stuffiness of her tiny room. She dismantled her bed bit by bit and heaved it downstairs into her study.

Instead of feeling more worried, Jim was furious. She'd already made her statement by leaving his bed. How much more pain did she need to inflict on him?

He now saw Nan as solely responsible for their continued lack of mutual understanding. Why couldn't she realise that his friendship with Charles was all to the good? Was a gateway to mending their fractured lives?

In particular, because Nan had such a practical streak, he felt her coldness was deliberate. As though she needed a reason to blame him for the chasm of mistrust that yawned between them. While any tentative overture of friendship on his part was rebuffed. Also, like a man on a raft, he feared that with any false move on his part the waves of Charles's bitterness might resurface and throw them all overboard.

When Charles and he went to Rogan's, he always begged her to join them, but she'd pout like an angry child, as if to say, You don't really want me there, to interfere with your intimacies, your male-bonding, and she'd turn her back on him without a word.

The silence! The silent piano! This is what saddened them

most – yes, Charles, also. There's no answer to silence. She was wielding a powerful weapon. How long would she continue thus?

They had an appointment with a team from Limerick the following day, but Jim feared the other's aggression if he reminded him. Nan's new move had also made Charles edgy with him, and Jim felt the slender bridge they'd built between them crumbling away. However, they did go, and that evening they arrived home with two young couples – students with whom they'd been working. Nan was as usual in the kitchen preparing the tea.

'This is my wife, Nan. Nan McDonald.'

The younger of the two girls, a small keen creature, with ropy hair and spectacles too large for her face, extended her hand to this strange gaunt woman.

'Nan McDonald? Not *the* Nan McDonald? Why, I heard you play in Limerick early this year. I'm Josie, Josie Finch, and this is Anne O'Reilly. We are both studying in Limerick. And Jack's from Maynooth and Oisin, our guru, is from Cork.' She turned to the others. 'Isn't this amazing? I never thought I'd actually talk to you. I was so in awe of you.'

And the girl called Anne cut in, 'Your husband, Jim, has been such a help to us. I hope we are not intruding on your work?'

Nan stood looking at them. Her hair hung loose in tangled streaks of grey around the temples. She was wearing a cardigan with holes in the elbows and a brown tweed skirt. 'Excuse me,' she said, and left the room.

The visitors looked stricken. 'I'm sorry,' Josie mumbled, while Charles bustled about arranging the chairs and bringing out knives and forks. He had that angry glint that Jim dreaded.

'No, no.' Jim felt obliged to say something. 'She's not very well at the moment, a touch of the flu.'

Charles poured out the tea with unnecessary speed.

'No, don't be sorry.' Jim couldn't climb into explanations, nor could he bring himself to follow Nan out of the room. She is my wife, he thought, and there is nothing I can do. How could he recapture their love? It seemed just then like a boat that had slipped its moorings, and was getting further and further out of sight. But somehow I must stand by her, he thought, or everything will be lost.

That night, he couldn't sleep. He strained for noises about the house. Nan had once called it a lucky house. But where was the luck now? He felt it was running away, like sand through the alchemist's fingers. He and Nan had turned base metal into gold, but how easily it tarnished. And he could not *only* blame Charles for the tragedy. And it was a tragedy. The stamp of genealogy had lodged itself in Charles's soul. It was as if Charles had emerged from a giant egg in which he had lain for thirty-one years and his emergence had destroyed his mother. He tossed on his lonely mattress. The duvet wound round his feet, the sheet buckled under him, and he knew that until he extricated himself from this paralysis he would never rest.

He got up and crept down to the kitchen. He padded like a ghost. Took down a glass and poured himself some whiskey. He drank it down and tiptoed down the corridor. At the door of Nan's study he tried to find his breath, but it came in little gasps. He put his hand on the handle and slowly turned it.

She was sitting up, her nightdress leaving one shoulder bare. Her eyes, hollowed and huge, tore his heart asunder. He cast about his mind for words to assuage his guilt. He longed to take her in his arms. To apologise for his neglect. To tell her he had hidden away from her because he was afraid. But that if only she would trust him now he could show her how all three of them could live in harmony.

'Talk to me, Nan, please,' he begged.

'Why did you bring them here? Why? Why didn't you tell

them they can see such creatures in St Jude's, catatonic waifs, cast-outs, with holes in their stockings and shoes with broken heels, allowed to wander the grounds doped and confused. Whose eyes don't focus any more. Yes.' She threw herself out of the bed, shuffling her feet into her slippers. 'You might have warned me. Don't ever do that again.'

He tried to say, sorry, but he was numbed by her onslaught. He licked his parched lips and followed her out of the room. She was taking the stairs two at time and they both tumbled together into their bedroom.

'Charles is as worried about you as I am,' was all he could think of saying.

'Oh, sure. Why don't you wake him and bring him here for a gawk?'

'But what's the matter? Why don't you tell me? Unless we talk, how can anything ever be solved?'

Ignoring him, she began to rummage in the chest of drawers.

'You heard what the girl said. She was in awe of you, admired you so much, never expected to have the privilege of meeting you. You heard her, Nan. Look at me.'

'Lucky for her!'

She kept on rummaging, bringing out make-up and combs. 'Hand me the nail clippers. On the beside table. And don't imagine, for one minute, I'm going to start playing. I just don't like the look of them any more.' She held up her hands, turning them this way and that. She began pulling out garments and strewing them on the floor. She finally selected a striped shirt, a pair of jeans and her smart high-heeled boots that had lain hidden for months. 'Now,' she said, 'give me the car keys.'

'No.'

'Jim, I said give me the car keys.'

He wanted to call Charles, who might make her see sense, and he barged out of the room, scared stupid, and shook

Charles awake. The latter, dragged from sleep, stumbled after him. But not even he could find words for Nan, this woman who for months had refused to speak to him. Why would she listen to him now?

And she sat brushing her hair, which she twisted into a bun and, taking a comb, twirled on to the top of her head. She carefully made up her eyes and then smiled at herself in the mirror. 'Now next time you bring your itsy-bitsy students into my house I won't be there to greet them. And don't worry about the car keys, I found them in your pocket.'

As the roads unpeeled, her body loosened. Her heartbeat slowed down. She was out on the main road now, her head-lights, picking up details on the empty highway, quietened her disordered thoughts. Her self-betrayal, her recent humiliations, she tried to put into focus as she concentrated on speed. She cast her mind to the time when Jim had driven out into the night and that he hadn't been able to sustain his anger, had limped home. She shook her shoulders, leaning a little forward over the wheel. She must try to remember the past few months. She could not remember single days, whether it had been cold or mild, whether the ground had frozen, whether the cows had calved. The two men, her husband, Jim, her son, once Séan now Charles, seemed to have occupied an alien section of her brain. Why had her mind cleared suddenly?

As she swerved to avoid a cat she said aloud, 'Séan is my son.' Yes. She had certainly borne him. She had wandered the hospital where Charity had sent her – the back end of the maternity wing, where the waifs bundled together. Kids with huge terrified eyes peeping out from under the grey cast-off army blankets. Blankets as coarse as turf. Angry midwives running from scream to scream. Slapping faces, pulling and ordering, lift, pull, breathe, until finally: Push. And each scarlet infant was drawn from a mother, held upside down and slapped. Another girl/mother's pain had ended.

She steadied her driving; she must not enter that corridor again. She was on the road. On the road once more. This was the important thing. Her piano? Can it wait for her? Stay there absorbing light? She wasn't ready yet, she knew, but somewhere, somewhere under her ribs, there was a small seam of hope.

She drove on and reached St Stephen's Green in the small hours. She parked the car at the corner and entered the Shelbourne.

The night porter in his purple waistcoat was bloated from lack of sleep.

Name? Nanny Wine. She filled in the form and took the lift up to No. 106. She laid her bag on the bed and drew the curtains back to watch a yellow streak gradually widening over the eastern end of the Green. She would soon see the corner of Leeson Street and Earlsfort Terrace, soon see the long grey building that had once been University College Dublin and that was now the National Concert Hall. She unpacked her bag and lay down to sleep.

The two men sat huddled in their dressing gowns as the dawn crept through the leaves of the chestnut tree.

'It's May Day tomorrow,' Jim said.

'The first of May.'

'Today I mean.'

Finally they were reduced to telephoning Swann. It was noon when he arrived, and the three men went into Nan's study, as though drawn by her fugitive spirit. Some music sheets lay on the floor where Nan must have flung them. Jim sat down on the piano stool while the other two stood.

'Yes,' Swann said. 'Delayed shock syndrome.'

'At meeting me.'

'More like giving you away.'

'I don't believe it.' Charles paced. 'No.'

'Soldiers get it. Often years later.'

Jim muttered, 'The hawthorne is in flower. Her favourite time of year.'

'I didn't know what I wanted when I came here.'

'Revenge,' Swann snapped.

Charles tried to explain that when they met in Crowsfort, Nan seemed to be trying to be something she wasn't. 'I had fantasised about her for so long. I wanted someone strong, who would drag me out of myself. And she was indecisive, afraid. And I was reminded of Victoria, not in looks – God, no – but in her lack of balance. I wasn't looking for a mother but this dark woman, what I called in my ignorance a career woman, threw me out of kilter. I could find nothing to say to her, I became aggressively tongue-tied.'

'How can anyone know how to cope with a situation like that? Of course Nan was terrified,' Swann interrupted.

Charles picked up the music sheet, turning to Jim. 'You seemed both so perfect when I came here. It was hideous. I had come from somewhere where all emotions were tidied away and here everything was bland, laid-back. I hadn't intended to, but I immediately reacted by putting on the armour of defiance. Something I was well practised in. I wanted *her* to react angrily. So that she'd ...'

'Love you?' Swann felt his own anger beginning to surface. 'An excuse for another breakdown?'

'I don't think so.' Charles walked across to Swann. 'I myself find it hard to understand. It was as if we were being hurled over the rapids of a turbulent river with no possibility of regaining momentum, of finding a purchase on dry land.'

'So you looked to Jim as a surrogate father. The most big-hearted man I know. If weak,' Swann added. He wanted to leave to attend to his patients. Children with earaches, old people with bronchitis. Something that could be cured by a simple prescription of antibiotics.

'And suddenly –' ignoring Swann – 'after that terrible row on Boxing Day, I was hit by an extraordinary feeling. A *déjà-vu*, you could call it. One day during those empty months she happened to come into the kitchen carrying a dish in both hands which she handed to Jim, no expression on her face. And my brain made a click. I'd seen this exactly before. Thinking about it afterwards, I knew what it meant, just as you know uncannily what some dreams mean. I had felt my body leaving her hands as she handed me over to Victoria and I knew, if she had kept me, I'd have loved her unconditionally. That's why, perhaps, I turned to Jim. Because he loved her unconditionally.' Charles had begun to pace around, picking up objects and putting them down. Stopping mid-tracks to swirl on Swann. 'I know what depression is. The Big D, we call it over there. And we, two average intelligent men, just slid past it. Wanted it out of the way.'

Jim, like a hunched monkey, chin in hands, elbows on his knees, gazed beseechingly at Charles, willing him to stop but unable to say a single word that might deliver him from the cartwheel of despair on which he was spinning. Finally he clapped his hands over his ears, shouting, 'Leave it, Charles, for God's sake leave it.'

Relentless, Charles continued, 'Dr Swann, I think what has happened here is way beyond your comprehension.' He put his hand on Jim's shoulder, nodding towards the door.

The three men shuffled out into the kitchen, where Jim grabbed the bottle of whiskey and poured them all a measure.'

'I don't drink before six,' Swann said icily, and left the house.

They tried all the main hotels but no Nan McDonald had checked in. No. All the night porters had gone off. Finally Jim flung down the phone. 'We can't check every fucking hotel in Ireland.'

In this way they dragged on, Charles in some instinctive way, taking over. Jim, in this torpid state, occasionally asking questions like, 'Do you not wonder about your father?' And when Charles shrugged, 'Well,' Jim recoiled. How could he admit that Nan had refused to tell him. That she could no longer trust him.

PART VI

AFTER A WEEK JIM HAD RUNG EVERY HOSPITAL in Dublin, and checked the guards for the car registration, but the latter came up with nothing. With meaningless optimism, they said they would find it eventually. 'Supposing she's driven it into a river or the sea?' Jim shouted at them, and Charles had to pacify him before he broke the phone up.

Charles went to Keveney's, the local mechanic, and bought an old car. He suggested they do something. Anything. Even whip up some of their old enthusiasms. 'There were several places you hadn't taken me to.'

'Oh, for fuck's sake,' Jim retorted. 'We should have talked. To her. It's my wife. And she has left me. Not you, you bastard.'

They wavered each side of the chasm again. Teetered on the verge of a physical fight. But Jim slid back. They were standing by the new car like two foolish schoolboys. He looked at Charles. 'Sorry. Yes, I am sorry.' He got into the driver's seat, saying, 'Let's go.'

Days passed without news. Charles turned his attention to the garden. He dug it and sowed the seeds. He pruned a neglected apple tree and tidied the raspberry canes. He put a clutch of eggs under a broody hen. By June the first row of lettuces were showing, and also the broad beans. His vegetables beds were as straight as a ruler and there wasn't a weed to be seen. Jim only left the house to feed the cows and passed Charles, head down, as though he were at something illegal. Most of the time he was drunk, starting the day with a large shot of whiskey, by evening fogged over with self-pity. He was tetchy with Charles, or worse still, like an old person, pleading for attention. Charles kept his distance, cleaning and cooking, but saw to it that Jim tried to eat, as if, indeed, he were minding his own father. But once he made the mistake of hiding one of the bottles, which resulted in Jim's throwing a hideous tantrum and tearing the place asunder, screaming at Charles to fuck off back to England and leave him alone.

Jim became slovenly. A heavy smell of unwashed clothes and stale booze pervaded the house. In bed he tossed and turned, tortured by hideous dreams. His grandfather, not the kindly old man he remembered, appeared to him like a monster trying to drag the corpse of his mother out of her grave, and he woke up, screaming, 'Don't, don't, don't.'

His body seized up and became full of wind. Stale farts issued from him as he tottered out to the field. He began to see Nan's silhouette in different places. Once, looking through the window of her study, he was sure he saw her. He ran in shouting, 'Nan. Oh, Nan,' only to find a chair had cast the shadow of a figure on the wall. The shock to his nerves attacked his stomach. He leant against the doorframe and vomited.

All day he sat at the bottle, the contents slowly dwindling as he lifted the last drops with his shaking hand. Afraid to go to the pub, he sent Charles out on errands for replacements for the precious drink. He lived in a tunnel of bewilderment from one glass of whiskey to the next.

He slept little and was usually up at five, cursing and breaking things if the whiskey had run out. Then it came when he could no longer stay still. He prowled the house, constantly looking over his shoulder. His mother's death began to crowd him, her yellowed hand trying to pacify him as he pulled at her bedcovers, till he screamed and drank from the neck of the bottle.

But one morning Charles, up around eight, was surprised to see Jim wasn't in the kitchen. He called upstairs, and when he got no reply he ran up into the room, his heart thumping. The bed was empty, grey sheets sagging over the mattress. The unmistakable smell of urine made him gag.

Of course. The car! It no longer stood where he had parked it the previous night. The quarry! He raced out of the house, down the road, the breath tearing out of him. At last a car came and he flagged it down. At the quarry the two men gazed down at the unrippled surface of the water beneath them, the shale sliding beneath their feet.

As the train crawled into Connolly Station the travellers began putting on their coats, dragging their bags off the rack and screwing up the rubbish of Coke bottles, sugar sachets, banana skins, and all the remains of what had been consumed during the boring four hours of travel. They stood eagerly in rows, like dogs who are promised a walk, as the *clack-clack* of the wheels crossed the points and sidled up to the platform. No one paid attention to a man crumpled against the window of a smoking compartment, apparently asleep.

An hour later, the contract cleaners arrived to clear up the mess before the train would be shunted off. They swept down the train with their bin bags, shovelling everything away.

Jim was snoring lightly when they found him. An empty bottle of Jameson rolled at his feet. 'Get this cunt out a here.'

He was carted off to Bride Street garda station and from there to the Mater Hospital.

When he came to the next morning he met the eyes of a cynical nurse.

'Where the fuck am I?'

A consultant was doing the rounds with his team of doctors. He turned to the nurse, who stood motionless as a plaster cast beside him. He muttered something Jim couldn't catch and she nodded. They passed on their way, poking their heads back and forth like a troupe of servile geese.

The nurse came back in and began to tidy up.

'I have to go now,' he said. She stood ominously looking down at him. 'I want my clothes.' His lips were so parched he could barely speak.

'Dr Nehru will talk to you later.'

As she walked away, he tried to shout, 'This is a free country, I believe,' but the words ran away as though buried in gravel.

It must have been about midnight when the doctor arrived. Surprisingly, she was a woman. She came in with her white coat open, her medical accoutrements swinging around her. She had vigilant brown eyes, slightly bloodshot at the rims. She picked up his wrist and her nails became khaki-coloured as she held his pulse. She put a thermometer in his mouth and left him to look at another patient.

'Can I go now?' he said when she came back.

She was shaking the thermometer to put back in a top pocket. She smiled. A cloud of musky perfume wafted round him as she bent down to write in her report.

'Where are you from?'

'Jaipur.'

'My great-grandfather went to India to work on the railways.' He lifted his head. 'He never came home.'

'You have pneumonia.'

He lay back, pinned down with astonishment and fever.

Charles found the car at the station. Sat at the telephone. Hotels, no. But yes, a Jim McDonald had been admitted to the Mater Hospital at 11.45 the previous day. He was in the medical ward. Could he come to the phone?

'I have to drag this cunting yoke around with me. I'm attached to a tube. On wheels. Are the cows all right?'

Charles told him he'd better get his arse home and not be

farting around on a wild-goose chase. 'You sound cheerful,' he added.

'I haven't had a drink for twenty-four hours. They've been injecting me with vitamin B and antibiotics. I feel like a telegraph pole that's been hit by a bus. All wires zinging. I've been hallucinating. I had to do an exam on astro-archaeology and I slaved and slaved at figures. It was awful.' There was a silence. 'Charles, are you there?'

'I'll ring you tomorrow.'

'God, don't go.'

Jim stood by the dead telephone. A man on crutches was queuing up behind him.

'Sorry.'

He went back to the ward.

Everything was spick and span in the kitchen as he feebly sat looking at Charles.

'Thanks.'

'Don't do that again. You frightened the guts out of me.'

After a week or so, his strength returning, he suggested they go to the pub for 'just the one'.

Reluctantly Charles got into the car.

'Long time no see.' Matt Rogan put the telly on full blast.

After two pints, Jim said, 'I should have gone looking for her. Dublin isn't that big.'

Slowly but surely, his intake of drink increased as each night he dragged Charles out. He knew the signs but was too scared to heed them.

Gradually he sank back into his torpid state, unheedful of the other's warnings. If anything he became more dishevelled, often jumbling his sentences in his efforts to seem in control.

Charles, trying to ignore him, continued to tend the garden, even feeding the animals, the one thing, he felt, that had anchored Jim to reality. The latter spent most of the day in the kitchen, making idiotic attempts at conversation, sometimes repeating the same joke and dribbling like a derelict.

Charles searched in his mind for a catalyst, something that could drag him to his senses. But strangely enough a change came about him through a kind of osmosis. One night Jim had a clear, untrammelled dream. He had bumped into Nan in the supermarket. Her trolley had been laden down and he took it from her and both of them went to the checkout, their plans full of the forthcoming meal. When he woke he burst into sobs, stuffing the sheet into his mouth, his body bucketing under the bedclothes. He screamed for Charles, his voice fluted with fear, and the latter came pounding up the stairs. Seeing Jim in this frenzied condition, he knew he had only one choice. To get the form signed and get him into hospital.

In the ambulance Jim clutched Charles's arm, while great ripples of shivers rolled over and over him. He had lost all control of his body. He felt the pee trickling away from him.

'It's all right,' Charles murmured, seeing the other's poor beseeching expression.

A vein was throbbing on Jim's forehead as he tried to lick the inside of his cheek where he had bitten it. And when he tried to sit up his body started shaking anew.

PART VIII

PREFABS HAD BEEN BUILT ON TO THE MAIN HOSPITAL and it was in one of these that Charles found Jim the following day. 'The detox wing,' Jim said, attempting a smile. 'And not a shrink in sight.' As his eyes closed over Charles noticed how emaciated Jim had become. It would be some weeks, he knew, before Jim could come home. He tucked the blankets round the other's chin, laying the back of his hand for a moment against Jim's cheek. He got quietly up and left the ward.

Gradually Jim's strength began to return. In between Charles's visits he played pool with, as he called them, other lunatics. He ate voraciously of the indifferent fare and Charles had to bring him apple tarts and fruit by the pound. He was bored stiff.

On his first visit home he sat in the kitchen, looking out the window at Charles, who had just mowed the lawn. The grass shone like steel. 'Charles,' he shouted. 'Charles, please come in.'

Charles laid down the hoe he was using along the ridges and, wiping his dirty hands on his trousers, walked into the kitchen.

'Tell me what to do, Charles. The meadow is growing, Charles, but I'm cold.' He looked up into the other's healthy features. He smelled the mown grass on the sleeve of his shirt.

'She called you Séan. Did that mean something? Tell me, please.'

'She told me about another girl. A girl called Elsie. A cockney. She told me she loved her. She said Elsie wanted to keep her baby.'

'She told me that, too.'

'Make some coffee, Charles ... Séan. . . . and sit down.'

They sat at the table drinking. Stirring their cups.

'Do you think she's dead?'

'No.'

'Will she ever come back?'

'Yes.'

'Nan is very sane. I thought it could go on for ever. My passion for this place.' He muttered about how they had always planned to leave the city. The excitement as they'd searched Ireland. Like two kids exploring a new hiding place. 'And when we found the house it was like a pledge. That Nan would continue, going and coming from her concerts, and I'd always be here to welcome her home. At the airport, terrified of the landing plane or, worse still, feeling my pelvis drop as it took off.' He fell silent. 'Why are you here, Charles? Why are you not chasing some woman? Surely you go mad for affection, like any normal person? What about sex? You lived with a woman once, I believe. Did it not feel good, touching the clitoris, curling your fingers round someone else's pubic hair? Feeling the softness of her belly, the hollow between the pelvic bones. Why are you doing this to me? Making me feel ashamed?' He reached for the bottle, but Charles drew his hand away.

'You've noticed the sun, Jim, for the first time in weeks. Easy. It's over, Jim, it's over,' and he picked him up and took him in his arms.

When July came Nan moved to a smaller hotel, an anonymous

one in the suburbs. During the day she came into town and toured the streets, wandering into cafés and galleries. She was afraid to go to exhibitions or concerts in case she was recognised.

From time to time she wondered about her house and the two men, and hoped they were surviving. She bore them no ill any more, but she knew she wasn't ready to go home. Might never be. Now that her balance had returned, or seemed to have returned, she wondered what had happened over those awful months. She tried to measure events, Jim's gradual change of heart, his burgeoning friendship with Charles, but there were still blanks in her memory. So, unbeknownst to herself, it was she who had had the nervous breakdown. All she remembered was that she and Charles had fought. And then after weeks, months, in that hideous void she had suddenly become what? A mother? A wife? Why? To expiate her guilt? Not that. Something to do with anger. And anger, the psychologists say, is good. But no, she could not go home yet. She kept the vision of Jim in the corner of her mind. Something sweet, valuable, like a cut stone. She must remain in Dublin incognito until the time was right.

She gradually made friends. A young artist became interested in her. For a while she toyed with the notion of going out with him. She went to his house in a small working-class street on the north side. He told her he was gay but if she liked he could manage. For the first time for months, it seemed, she burst into laughter.

'If only you knew!'

They made tea and watched the telly.

They became friends. Like two heroes. Survivors of society. She would arrange to meet him at the theatre or the cinema, after which they'd go somewhere for a meal. They laughed a lot. She might have stayed on like that, letting things slide, if it hadn't been that one day he persuaded her to go to an opening, where she was finally recognised. When he realised who she was, he was hurt.

'What's with all the secrecy?'

So she'd have to go further afield. She thought of going to London for a spell, where no one would know her, so she booked a flight and landed one evening at Heathrow. At first she had a crazy notion of going to look for Elsie. To trawl London for the one person who now seemed her only anchor. But she knew that time brings different rewards to different people. Elsie would be strong now, living with or near her grown-up daughter. Her life in order. And where would she start to look? In that teeming metropolis ... She probably would have married. Changed her name.

She wandered into the underground and, reaching London, went to Charing Cross station and took the train to Hindhead. Without thinking, she found herself in Crowsfort. She went to the post office and inquired about a Jasper Fordson, who might live near. That Uncle Jasper Charles mentioned. He hadn't said he was dead. So once more she was walking up that village street and checking in at the Wheatsheaf.

They told her that he lived not far away. She hired a taxi and went to the address. This man, in his late seventies or eighties, had a sad face like a discarded purse. The skin was pitted all over with russet markings. He stood in the wedge of the half-open door.

'Mr Fordson?' He stuck out his lower lip.

'What is it?' There was a tremor in his voice. He pushed his spectacles further up his nose, revealing a bronze spot on the back of his hand like a medal.

She wondered if she was suitably dressed, as she had wondered a year ago when she went to meet Charles. 'I'm a friend of Charles, your nephew. Can I come in?'

Surprisingly, he opened the door a little wider and pattered back down the hall.

'Yes, yes.'

'I've just come to send you his greetings.' She walked after him uncertainly.

The shabby corridor ended in a door, through which he led her. Charles's past loomed out at her. Thus had he lived down his childhood years. Now she knew he hadn't lied. His, or what she thought might be his, exaggerations fell into the jigsaw of time. The room they entered was a dusty replica of the one into which Charles had taken her. Another cheaply framed picture, this time of a horse and cart, hung over the mantelpiece and a window facing north was shrouded by a heavy beech tree. It was dusk in the room although it was still sunny outside. The old man fussed at his lapels. 'Have they shut him up? Have you come from the hospital?'

She wanted to leave immediately. There was nothing here for her. No clue.

'No, he's in Ireland.'

He looked puzzled. 'My brother did everything for that boy.'

Nan saw the film reeling backwards. What abominable luck. They could have been wonderful. Full of sun and noise. She heard Miss Charity's voice. A respectable couple. Special, they said you wanted them. So she had handed him over to this brumous life, where the sun never shone and the air never penetrated. No, he hadn't won the lottery after all.

As she turned to go, he stepped in front of her. 'Don't leave,' he said petulantly. 'I have visitors so seldom. Please sit down.' As though pushed from above, she sat. It was a straight-backed chair with a frayed satin built-in seat. A Queen Anne copy, fashionable in the 1950s.

When would he tell her about the bad blood? Should she prompt him? But what he said was, 'A terrible business.'

She was grateful. He must be talking about the accident. 'Yes, dreadful to lose both parents at once.'

'Of course, they weren't his parents. He was whelped by some girl who gave him away.' He took off his specs to clean them with a soiled-looking handkerchief, while he blew out his cheeks. 'I warned Jack, but of course Vicky was determined. Women's trouble,' he said mysteriously.

'Yes?'

'That woman, Vicky, persuaded Jack. Not a bad woman, if stupid. Didn't believe in the cane. Spoiled him. I did my best. Birthdays and Christmas.'

He doesn't go out, this man, she thought, needs to talk. So his tongue runs along: *tackety-tack, tackety-tack*. A train full of clichés.

'What was their house like? Jack and Vicky's?' He didn't understand the question. How could he? 'Have you photographs of your brother and his wife? I'd like to see them. If you have any.'

He went to a bureau and produced a bundle of snapshots. One showed a couple, the woman holding a large baby in christening robes.

She stared long at the photo. Here was the baby. Her baby. In a silly long dress. His head tucked into a bonnet.

The baby that she had willingly given to this very woman who held him in her arms . . . Frozen in time.

She gazed from the picture to the old man. She held it against her breast, wanting to touch his hand.

The man in the snapshot was a young copy of this Jaspar who stood before her. The same small round face, but clear and patient. The woman was angular, with short fuzzy hair, a thin nose and pointed chin, who looked sternly at the camera.

She wondered if he had ever had time to give her an orgasm. Steady, she kept saying to herself. Steady.

When words finally came, she asked him if she could keep it. She tried to hide the shake in her hand as she held the picture out to him. 'You see,' she stammered, 'I . . . I'll see him when I go home. And . . . And I know he'd like to have it.' He still seemed puzzled, so she finished lamely with, 'It was good of them to adopt a child. Give an orphan a home.'

He put the other photos back. She got up. 'Thank you for

seeing me. I'll tell Charles you're well. You are keeping well?' She held out her hand. 'He'll be glad to hear it. He speaks fondly of you.'

There was no irony in her tones, but as she turned, he said, 'You need some refreshment, a glass of sherry perhaps.'

'Please don't trouble. I'm sure you have things to do.'

He gave a short laugh. 'I sometimes trot down to the village for my meagre needs. Otherwise I have nothing to do.' He bustled to a cabinet and brought out two glasses and a half-full bottle.

She sat again to take the proffered glass. Why did he never marry, this worn creature? An old coat cast aside, 'trotting' back and forth for his bachelor food, tinned beans, packet soups, sliced bread allowed to go mouldy when only half-eaten. A piece of cheese in a silver wrapper, maybe a bit of leathery steak on Sundays. And the beech tree outside lush and green. Nothing to do with his life, only stifling it further.

Now she wanted something for him. Something to brighten Charles's past. An open car, taking them to Bournmouth in August. But all she saw were his fussy hands undoing the parcel at Christmas. A train set for a sixteen-year-old boy. And Jack and Vicky preparing the turkey without the cranberry sauce. Where was the laughter? Surprise? 'Always what I wanted? Thank you. Oh, thank you, Uncle Jasper?' She ran a finger over the smooth surface of the photo which she'd put in her pocket. The picture of three people taken outside a church.

And who was to blame? Nanny Wine? The wild black-haired one. Slinking up to the man with the Roman profile, her bra strap falling down her arm, running the back of her hand down the back of his, deliberately spilling her drink so he noticed her? That's what, not this poor old anachronism, not the prim Vicky and puzzled, patient Jack.

And not Nan McDonald the well known pianist. Nanny Wine, daughter of Louis Wine, and sister of fair-haired Lizzie and Sam, who had played on the step of the shop on days like this, cast aside her dolls to join the boys kicking ball in the Diamond, who had stood on the steps of the synagogue in Adelaide Road, after leaving her child in England, her secret a burden she would never throw on the shoulders of her family, and who to this day were ignorant of it.

And this isn't me here now. I'm really in Prague or Leipzig or Cork, wading my way through Bob Bailey's concerto, chancing the most difficult bits, hoping no one will recognise them. I can see the conductor bowing as if he'd played the whole score himself, hear the thunder of hands ricocheting against the walls.

'You must be lonely,' she said.

It was really dusk now. Not just that unnatural half-light that was his, all day long. She would walk back to the Wheatsheaf. Perhaps have a solitary drink.

'I'll tell Charles I met you.'

The Mean Wells, the Don't Knows, the Didn't Thinks. She was chastened. We're all the same.

'Don't get up.'

She left him sitting there, a victim of his brutal life, a life of respectability that had crushed him into a woodlouse under its wheels. Would he weep with loneliness when she left? No. Leave that to volatile people like herself and Jim, who gorged themselves on self-pity. Jasper Fordson would put away the sherry bottle, open a tin of Heinz tomato soup and sit down at his solitary table before putting on the TV to watch *Coronation Street* or the news.

That July evening the weather was unsettled. Every day it was the same. Cool, showery, unpleasant. Charles was working at the potatoes, earthing them up, and Jim was mending, for the millionth time, the galvanised roof of the shed. They both looked up when they heard the car.